FIC
BAWD

PROPERTY OF SCHOOL
DISTRICT NO. 75

FIC
BAWD

Bawden, Nina

Henry

DATE			
(Misha Jensen)			
11-15-07 (3)			
(rele)			

913

HENRY

ALSO BY NINA BAWDEN
The Finding
Kept in the Dark
The Robbers
Squib

HENRY

NINA BAWDEN

ILLUSTRATED BY
JOYCE POWZYK

LOTHROP, LEE & SHEPARD BOOKS
NEW YORK

First Edition 1 2 3 4 5 6 7 8 9 10

Library of Congress Cataloging in Publication Data
Bawden, Nina, (date) Henry.
Summary: Evacuated to the English countryside during World War II, a fa-
therless family tries to raise a baby squirrel that also lost its home. [1. Family
life—Fiction. 2. World War, 1939–1945—England—Fiction. 3. Squir-
rels—Fiction. 4.England—Fiction] I. Powzyk, Joyce Ann, ill. II. Title.
PZ7.B33He 1988 [Fic] 87-29339
ISBN 0-688-07894-X

*In memory of my mother, Judy Mabey,
who kept alive this story of Henry,
and for Sam, Matthew, Ottilie, and David,
who are too young to have heard her tell it.*

HENRY

O N E

My brothers, Charlie and James, have always blamed me for what happened to Henry. Even now, years and years later, Charlie still says it was my fault. The cage was to keep Henry *in,* not (as our mother had told me) to keep people *out.* I suppose everyone always has a different story to tell. This is mine. At least, it is what I remember. . . .

In fact, in a way, it was *Charlie's* fault! Sharp-eyed Charlie, who had spotted the nest high in the tree by the brook; who watched for a while, several days, and then fetched his friends, Tommy and Stan, and his big brother's slingshot. A lucky shot for a little boy only seven years old, though not so lucky, of course, for the squirrels. As James said when Charlie came home with his prize, "How would *you* like it? If someone blew *your* house to bits and spilled you out in the cold?"

Charlie went red and then white. (This was a long time ago, in the war. The house at the end of our street in London had been bombed in the Blitz, blown to smithereens along with everyone in it. Charlie had heard the bomb fall, and although it was three years now since we had left the city to live on this farm in the country, he still jumped and went pale when a tractor backfired or Mr. Jones, the farmer, was out shooting rabbits.)

"You're as bad as Hitler," James said.

"I'm— —not."

"*Charlie!*" our mother said.

"— — —!"

"Don't swear, Charlie!"

Charlie was the most terrible swearer. He looked so sweet, with his pink-and-white angel face and big, innocent eyes, but he never opened his mouth without cursing. It wasn't wickedness. Charlie didn't understand what he was saying. He was just copying Bill, the farm cowman, who didn't seem to know any words *except* bad ones. Charlie loved to trot around after Bill, helping to muck out the cowshed, waving a stick and banging the cows on their fat rumps when Bill fetched them for milking, and shouting the same dreadful names that Bill called them. Names that I can't repeat. *Blank, blank, blank,* is how they are written in books, and that was how my small brother talked. *Blank, blank, blankety-blank.*

Our mother tried to stop him, of course. She used to fine him. Some weeks he lost all his pocket money. But she didn't fine him this time. She was too interested in the tiny squirrel he had tugged out of his pocket. The squirrel was about three inches long, very ragged and skinny. "I've *blankety* well got the *blank, blank* nest, too," he said proudly.

"Give the poor baby to me," our mother said. She curled it in her broad palm and cupped her other hand over it. "Peace and quiet's what he needs."

"Charlie ought to put it back," James said.

"Too late for that."

"It's cruel."

"No it's *blank* not," Charlie said. "It's *blank* nature study."

"That's enough, Charlie," our mother said. "Go and get a cardboard box and some hay from the barn. And leave the nest on the table."

Charlie went. James and I prodded the nest with our fingers. It had got a bit squashed inside Charlie's jacket but it still held together; a tangle of sticks and grass with a lining of moss and leaves and some sort of tree bark. I said, "A squirrel's nest is called a drey,

3

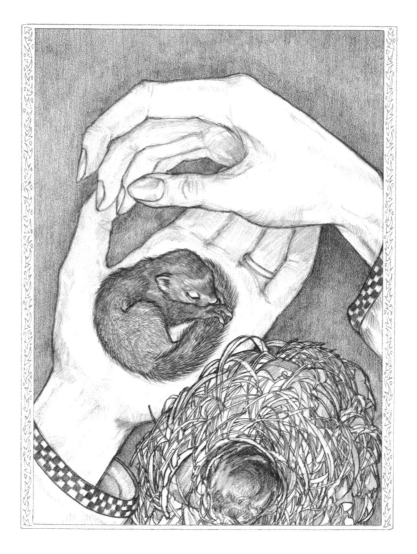

isn't it? There would have been more than one baby, wouldn't there?"

"I saw Charlie in the lane with Tommy and Stan," our mother said. "I expect they each took one."

"Horrible boys! Poor little squirrels."

"You're not sorry Charlie brought one home for us, are you?" It was plain that *she* wasn't sorry! She was bright with excitement!

"We'll be sorry if it dies," James said. "Will it die?"

"Not if we look after it properly."

Our mother was good at looking after things. Orphaned lambs and baby calves on the farm, and wild creatures, too. Last summer she had nursed a hare with a broken leg and she always put out bread and milk for the hedgehogs. James said that she even fed the fat spider in the privy down the garden with dead flies and beetles. I wasn't sure that I believed him, but it was certainly possible. She was mad about animals. Sometimes I thought that she preferred them to people. Except for Charlie, of course; her baby, her favorite.

He flung the door wide and came crashing in with a big box of dusty hay. She tucked the nest into it and let the squirrel go. It disappeared instantly. There was a tiny rustle as it shot into the hay and then stillness and silence.

We all sat around. Nothing happened. Not a

squeak, not a flick of a whisker. We didn't move either. Even Charlie stayed quiet as a mouse—or as quiet as our squirrel—until it began to grow dark outside.

He said, "I'm *blank* hungry."

Our mother went to get supper ready, and James and I fixed the blackout frames over the windows and lit the oil lamps; the small Tilley lamp in the kitchen, and the hanging brass lamp over the table in the sitting room. The Tilley lamp had to be pumped and made a steady hissing noise once it got going. The hanging lamp was harder to start, but once the yellow flame was turned down and burning blue around the wick, it gave a gentler, more golden light than the Tilley.

Although there was electricity in the barn and the cowshed there was none in the house, and we were used to being without it by now, just as we were used to pumping up every drop of the water we needed for drinking and cooking and washing from the well in the yard and carrying it indoors in buckets, and going down the garden to the earth closet, and living in one room and a kitchen instead of a whole house as we had done in London. None of these things was any hardship to us. The room we rented on the first floor of the farmhouse was big enough to take all the furniture we had brought with us, and, except for meals, we were not often in it. There was too much to be seen and too much to do on the farm.

Most evenings after supper while Charlie was being bathed in a tin bath in front of the fire, James and I went to help with the milking or to shut up the chickens for Mrs. Jones. Or, if there were no jobs to be done, we'd just hang about in the barn or the wagon shed with the Joneses' son, Abel, who was about the same age as we were—a bit older than James, a bit younger than me. But tonight neither of us wanted to budge.

Nor did the squirrel, though we waited and waited. Our eyes itched and watered with waiting.

"Bed," our mother said. Charlie was already asleep in the big bed he shared with her in one corner of the huge room. James and I slept on camp beds in the apple room on the other side of the landing, where apples were laid out in rows to keep through the winter, and rats and mice scuttered at night, overhead in the attics.

"It's not fair," we said. "The squirrel might wake."

"Bed," she said.

"If it wakes, Charlie will see it before us."

"Bed."

We hated her, but we went. In the morning, before even Bill was up (usually the first thing we heard was him swearing and stamping up the yard in his stiff, heavy boots), we raced into the room. Charlie was already sitting at the table eating his breakfast.

"Is he alive?" James said.

A look passed between Charlie and our mother. A self-conscious smirk.

She said, "He's all right. Eat your breakfast."

"You've *looked*," I said. "Haven't you? You wouldn't let us look last night, but you've looked this morning."

She said, "Breakfast first."

I swallowed my hot porridge so fast my throat burned. James choked on his and made sick-sounding noises.

"Oh, leave it, leave it," she said, impatiently, as if *she* couldn't bear to wait any longer.

She put some pieces of bread in the box, just in front of the hole in the hay. The hay stirred. There was a small, nibbling sound. A furry head poked out. I saw its dark, beady eyes, its sharp-pointed ears.

I said, "Squirrels have hair sticking out of their ears. His are bare. Like a rat's. And he's sort of brown. I thought squirrels were gray."

"London squirrels," she said. "Not this one. He'll be red when he's grown. And he's too young yet to have tufts in his ears. Do you think he wants a drink? Shall I teach him to suck, like we do with the calves?"

She dipped her finger in the milk she had warmed for our porridge and held it in front of the squirrel. There was a very faint rasping sound as it started to suck. She said, "What shall we call him?"

"Ssh," James said. "Don't speak so loud, Mum. You'll scare him."

8

She laughed. "Scared is the last thing he is!"

As if he had understood what she said, the squirrel came out of the hay at that moment and sat on the edge of the box. Squirrels don't have much expression in their faces, but his eyes seemed alert and inquisitive, as if he were as interested in us as we were in him.

"Squirrels are supposed to be born in May or June," our mother said. "That's what the books say. It shows you books don't know everything. March the twenty-second today, and he's about four or five weeks old, I'd guess, with those tuftless ears and that raggedy tail. He looks as if he wants to play. Why don't you pick him up, one of you?"

And one of us did. I can't remember who was bold enough to be first, only that we passed him from hand to hand, stroking him rather timidly, until we found out that what he seemed to be asking for was quite a rough game; rolling on his back while we tickled his stomach and he fought with his feet, kicking our hands with his back legs, clinging to our fingers with his front paws, with his little stumpy thumbs and long toes. He chattered and nipped with his teeth; very gentle nips, as if he knew that he mustn't bite.

"He's tame!" James said, but it wasn't quite that. It was more as if he had never been wild, as if he had never lived in a nest in a tree with his family. Tipped out of his old life, as we had been tipped out of ours when the bombing got bad and we had to leave London, he was at home in his new life from the beginning; as at home in our sitting room as we were at home on the farm.

"I expect he just thinks we're some new kind of tree," Charlie said, so interested that for once he managed to speak without swearing.

"Why should he be frightened? It's not natural for living creatures to be afraid of each other," our mother said. She really believed this. She was never frightened of animals; not of strange dogs as I was, nor even of the Hereford bull on the farm, as she ought to have been. "Remember that little shrew James found in the wheat field last August? He wasn't scared either. He ran all over us."

"He died," James reminded her. "We didn't feed him the right things and he died. What are we going to feed this squirrel on? Squirrels eat nuts and we haven't got any. You can't buy them in the shops because of the war and they won't be ripe on the trees till the autumn."

His voice trembled suddenly; his face had gone pinched and pale with anxiety. James worried more than the rest of us about almost everything. I saw our mother frown as she looked at him. But her voice was sturdy and cheerful. "Squirrels have to make do like the rest of us. He doesn't seem fussy so far. He's had bread and milk. We'll try bits of this and that. Apples. Corn. Porridge. Some of that left this morning,

10

I've noticed! Meantime the poor baby needs sleep."

He was asleep already, in fact; worn out by the roly-poly game, lying on my knee, flat on his stomach, legs stretched out in front and behind. But our mother was longing to hold him herself. "Come along, Henry," she said, scooping him up and tucking him inside the neck of her sweater. "Time for your nap."

"Henry?" James said. "Is that what we're calling him?"

"I had a great-uncle called Henry. He looks a bit like him."

"Do you mean our squirrel looks like your great-uncle or your great-uncle looks like our squirrel?"

"Bit of both. They look like each other."

"It's a funny name for a squirrel. It makes him sound like a person."

"Do you think that he isn't?"

I said, "We don't even know if it is a *he*, do we?" I had had a good look while I tickled his tummy but I hadn't seen anything.

"Oh, you would ask that, wouldn't you, Miss?" our mother said, pretending to sigh. "Questions, questions! If you haven't got anything better to do, I have, I can tell you! I'd have thought you'd have wanted to be out and about this fine, sunny morning, not hanging about indoors. Though if you want jobs, I daresay I can find them!"

We knew what *she* wanted!

11

"Don't suppose we'll get much to eat today," James said, as we clattered downstairs and out into the yard. "She'll be too busy playing with Henry."

"Why should she waste her time cooking for you? Greedy guts. Mr. Stuff-Your-Face."

"Shut up. You're the greedy one. *Fatty!*"

I caught his arm and twisted it up behind him. I said, "Say you're sorry."

"*Sorry.*"

I let him go and he rubbed at his elbow, pulling a face as if I really had hurt him. He said, "She'd be more interested in us if we were puppies or kittens."

"You wouldn't want her to fuss over you. She might make you wash your neck a bit oftener."

James shook his head and sighed.

I said, "She likes to have something small to look after."

"She's got Charlie."

"Oh, jealous, are you? I shouldn't bother. Charlie's not exactly cuddlesome any longer."

We heard Charlie's boots pounding behind us and jumped aside just in time. He came tearing past, swerving in front of us to charge through a lovely puddle that had cow pats and a blue shimmer of oil mixed up with the water, splashing it up over us as well as over his own short, stout, bare legs. "Bill," he was shouting. "*Bill*, wait for me."

James dabbed at what had been up to this moment a pair of fairly clean trousers. "About as cuddlesome as a charging rhinoceros," he said.

Bill's head rose up from behind the wall of the pigsty. He had been having a quick smoke after milking. "*Blank, blank,* yer little *blank,*" he yelled back at Charlie, grinning away, his red hair blazing around his kind, merry face and curling down over the old sack he wore draped on his shoulders.

James said, "I wish the war would end soon. I wish Dad would come home. He'd be good for Charlie. And I think Charlie misses him."

James meant that *he* missed him. Our father was at sea, in the navy. He was chief engineer on an armed merchant cruiser on patrol duty, escorting convoys of ships across the Atlantic; troop ships and cargo ships, coming and going between England and America, dodging the German submarines and the German battleships. We all missed him, but James missed him much more than Charlie, who barely knew him. In the last four years Dad had only been home on leave twice. And Charlie had Bill.

Bill was out from behind the sty now, and Charlie was racing up to him, grabbing his arm, hanging on to it. "Bill, listen you *blank,* I've got a *blank* squirrel called Henry."

T W O

Outside the cowshed, Abel was backing the white pony into the shafts of the trap, getting ready to take the churns up the narrow lane to the main road to meet the milk lorry. "I'll tell Abel," James said.

He ran to help lift the full churns off the stand. Charlie and Bill were getting the cows out of the shed. I could hear the rattle of their neck chains and Bill's big, gusty laugh.

I looked for someone to tell. Mr. Jones might be interested, though he wouldn't say much, never did. But he wasn't about; not in the wagon shed or up the farmyard. I saw Mrs. Jones's straw basket hooked on the gate of the chicken field, and knew that she hadn't picked up the eggs yet. Charlie and James ran in and out of the Joneses' kitchen whenever they felt like it, but I liked to have an excuse.

There were nine eggs in the nesting boxes; not bad, but with fourteen laying hens and only two of them broody, it should have been better. Mrs. Jones's favorite brown hen was coming up from the brook, stepping slowly and elegantly on her splayed yellow feet and chuckling softly; a conceited bird, very pleased with herself. I said, "I know what *you've* been up to!" and she cocked her head smugly.

Mrs. Jones was in the dairy; a long, cool room off her big, stone-flagged kitchen, banging and slapping away at her freshly churned butter, shaping it into neat pounds with two carved wooden pats that left a pattern of leaves and flowers. I counted the eggs into cartons and said, "Charlie came home with a baby squirrel last night. Mum says she's going to rear it."

Mrs. Jones made a clicking sound with her tongue; a bit amused, a bit disapproving. "Well, she's got a rare way with creatures. Though I hope she knows it's most likely verminous. Bound to have fleas. And a squirrel's bite is worse than a rat's. You should watch out for that, keep it shut up. There's an old birdcage up in one of the attics that belonged to my Auntie Blodwen. She had a pet thrush once that she took everywhere with her. Sing, sing, you never heard anything like it. Abel used to love that old bird when

he was a little lad. I reckon that's what started him singing himself, trying to copy it. Pity not to have Abel's voice trained, I've thought sometimes, but there's so much old work on a farm. If we'd had another boy to give Father a hand it might have been different. Thank you for getting the eggs, you're a good girl. Has that old brown hen started laying again?"

All the time she was talking she went on pounding the butter. She was a tiny, quick, delicate person who hardly ever stopped working and never stopped talking, hopping from one thing to another so fast it was sometimes hard to keep up with her.

I did my best. I said, "I don't think Henry's got fleas. If he has, Mum's got some flea powder. And I'll tell her about the birdcage. She says Abel's got perfect pitch, she knows about that sort of thing. She used to sing in the church choir when she was a girl. I think the brown hen is laying all right, though not in the boxes. She came cackling up, sounding sort of contented. I think she's got a nest hidden somewhere."

"We'll have to put salt on her tail," Mrs. Jones said. "Ever seen that done?"

I shook my head and she laughed; her bright blue eyes snapped with laughter. She covered the butter with cheesecloth, then took a crockery jar off the shelf and shook a little salt into her apron pocket. There was corn in a sack by the back door and she took a handful. "Now you'll see something," she said, sounding excited and eager—as eager as Charlie when he thought of some mischief. She was pale and thin—had grown paler and thinner since she had been in hospital this last winter—but she was so full of energy it was hard to believe she had ever been ill. "Mrs. Jones is all spirit," was what our mother said. I had to run to keep up with her as we went down the chicken field.

She scattered the corn and the greedy brown hen was the first to come pecking. Mrs. Jones scooped it up, tucked its head and neck under her arm, and reached for the salt in her apron. She rubbed her hand under the hen's tail and it made a fearful squawking. Mrs. Jones winked at me. "That should do it. Get a bit of salt right into her, where the egg come out. Sets up a bit of old irritation, see, makes her think she needs to lay another egg. Watch where she goes now."

She put the hen down, and it shook its feathers with an offended cackle and set off at once for the brook. I followed along the bank, past the sheep dip, past the muddy patch where the cows went down to drink sometimes, to a steeper part where thorny brambles grew down to the water. The hen squeezed under a low, scrubby bush. I slithered down after it, parted the branches, and saw the hen flutter away from the clutch of speckly eggs in their secret nest. "Never fails, see?" Mrs. Jones said, reaching down from the bank to give me a hand with the basket. "Silly bird! She's too old to be put in the coop to learn better. She'll have to go in the pot."

After three years on the farm, I knew better than to be shocked at the idea of eating a creature you knew and were fond of. I said, "Wouldn't she hatch the eggs out, if we left them?"

"Not that old hen. She's too flighty, not enough patience to sit. My fault, I daresay, for making a pet of her, letting her into the kitchen when she came scratching round the back door. Animals ought to be kept in their place, and that isn't inside a house. Except for a sick lamb, sometimes, or a good dog, or a bird in a cage."

"Or a baby squirrel?"

Mrs. Jones laughed and then coughed, her hand pressed to her side as if something there hurt her. She said, wheezing and laughing, "Well, if your mother doesn't mind it knocking her pretty things over, and scratching the furniture, and making its mess everywhere! Never heard of anyone house-training a squirrel! Still, if it makes your mam happy, that's good enough for me. I'm afraid she must find us rough country folk a bit dull sometimes. I expect she misses her smart London friends."

"She misses our father," I said. "No one else, far as I know."

As we walked back to the house I saw her standing at the window of our room and waved to her.

She didn't wave back because she wasn't looking down at the chicken field. She was looking straight ahead, above and beyond us, at the bare Welsh hills rising around the wide valley. I had often come into the room and found her like that, standing at the window and looking out, still and dreaming.

I said, "It's London that's dull. Just boring streets and streets of ugly, horrible houses."

I saw by Mrs. Jones's smile that she didn't believe me. She had never been to London and was quite sure that all the people there lived in palaces.

I said, "Mum always hated the city. She likes it much better here. Really she does. We all do. And you're all our best friends. You're Mum's best friend, and Abel is James's best friend, and Bill is Charlie's best friend." That seemed to leave me out, so I added, more for tidiness than truth, "And I suppose Mr. Jones is mine, really."

She tucked her bony hand under my elbow and pinched my arm. She gave a little snort of laughter, though I hadn't said anything funny. She said, "I daresay I can let you have a bit of corn for your squirrel."

He ate the corn. He lapped some milk from a saucer. He ate some bits of bread and half a crumbled-up biscuit. He did his best to eat sitting up. When he toppled over, he sat up again. He was very determined. We gave him a prune stone and he worked on it, cleaning it up until it looked as if it had been polished. Then we cracked it, and he ate the kernel.

"He'll be sick," James said. And he was, very neatly.

"Just returned what he can't cope with," our mother said, mopping up. "At least we don't have to worry about what he'll eat. He's omnivorous. Do you know what that means?"

"He'll eat anything," James said. "And this is the *holidays*, Mum. We're supposed to be resting our brains, not wearing them out playing word games. I think we ought to write to Dad and ask him to send us some nuts next time he goes ashore in America. Do you think Henry will eat apples? There's lots of squishy ones in the apple room. I don't think Mrs. Jones wants them."

"We'll find out," our mother said. "All in good time. Make a list, James, write everything down. Unless you're afraid it will put too much strain on your thinking equipment."

James started the list that evening in a small notebook with ruled lines and shiny black covers. He wrote HENRY'S FIRST DAY, and put down all he had eaten. Henry sat on the table, fairly steady now, and seemed to be watching. Then he made several small, tottering jumps, dancing backward and forward, and launched himself into the air. He landed on the edge of the box of hay that stood on a chair a little below him, dived into the hay, and vanished completely.

We waited as we had done the day before. Nothing happened. Our mother looked at her watch. "Half past seven," she said. "I do believe he's put himself to bed. Knows when he's had enough. Not like some I could mention."

We all groaned. James said, "I promised to show him to Abel."

"Tomorrow," she said. "Babies need sleep. You can show him to Abel first thing. He'll be nice and fresh in the morning."

But when we got up the next day, he was gone.

THREE

It was a beautiful morning; pale spring sunlight streaming in through the wide open windows, and birds singing their hearts out. Our mother was making porridge on the oil stove. She was wearing an old white shirt of our father's and humming softly to herself. She looked very cheerful and young. I said, "Where's Henry?"

"Sleeping tight, bless him."

"Have you looked?"

She shook her head, smiling. "You can get him up if you like. Only be gentle."

I felt in the hay. I said, "He's not there!"

She stopped smiling. I shouted for Charlie and

James and we searched the hay box in turn. We looked everywhere we could think of; under the bed, down the sides of the armchairs, under cushions. We sat glumly at the table and ate our breakfast porridge. It was lumpy and burnt, but no one complained. "I expect he fell out of the window," James said, at last. "I expect the cat got him."

Charlie went red in the face and swore at some length. Our mother sighed, but said nothing.

"I'm going out," James said. He picked up his jacket from the chair where he'd left it the night before, and put an arm into a sleeve. He started to giggle. Inside the sleeve and fast asleep was Henry.

He woke as bright as a button. He seemed pleased to see us. We put him on the table and he made a flying leap, landing on James's shoulder and dodging around the back of his neck, from side to side, to and fro, peeping at the rest of us as if he wanted us to play hide-and-seek with him. Charlie hopped up and down with excitement. "It's like I *blankety* well said! He thinks James is a *tree*!"

James was pulling agonized faces, screwing up his nose and his mouth, trying not to wriggle or squirm in case he frightened our baby. As we were all to find out, it wasn't easy being a tree, particularly when Henry decided to hurtle down the front of your shirt without warning and hunt for a comfortable, warm resting place next to your skin, or tuck a tasty morsel of food away in your armpit. Charlie got the worst of it. Like most small boys at that time, he wore baggy gray flannel shorts, nice and wide at the bottoms, very convenient for a squirrel to hide in. Charlie went *wild!* Henry didn't scratch, but he tickled terribly, and got mixed up with his underpants.

But this time we all just fell about laughing at James's tortured expressions, and Charlie laughed louder than anyone. We played hide-and-seek for a bit until Henry got bored with the game and made a jump for the table and the remains of our breakfast. He went straight to a jar of jam, standing up on his legs, reaching up to the sticky rim. "Naughty," our mother said. She put her hand round him, gently and carefully, and he made a little sound, the first we had heard from him, a kind of low purring. As she took him away from the jam jar, the sound became louder and clearer. Henry spoke his first words. "*Vut, vut, vut.*"

"He's angry," Charlie said. "He's swearing."

"Well, *you* should know!" our mother said.

"He only wanted a bit of jam," James said. "Do squirrels eat jam?"

It seemed that this squirrel did. We put him on the wide sill of the window that looked over the chicken field and fed him his breakfast; a bit of dry bread, milk and water to drink, a teaspoon of jam for a treat. He licked the spoon shining clean. Then he

25

sat up a bit unsteadily and started to wash himself, sweeping his tail through his fingers, cleaning the backs and fronts of his arms. He dropped a few pellets, like poppy seeds. Our mother brushed them out of the window. "Toilet training," she said. "Not much fuss about that. Good boy, Henry."

"Lucky boy, Henry," I said. "*We* have to go down the garden."

I didn't really mind the earth closet, except when it was raining hard or very dark. In fact, it was pleasant and airy inside, not too smelly, and the paper hanging from a nail on the inside of the door was cut-up pages from the *Dairy Gazette* or the *Farmer's Weekly,* so there was always something to read. There were three holes in the pale, seamed, wooden bench— large, medium, and small. If it was windy, paper and leaves would blow up from the two unoccupied ones while you were sitting there. Charlie complained about that; he was very fastidious. But the only thing I disliked, the thing that embarrassed me, was the way Abel and James sometimes teased me if they were around when I went there. They'd stand outside giggling and pretending that they wanted to go themselves, very badly. It was only boys' silliness, but it made me shy. Sometimes I hung about waiting until I got a pain.

This morning, James was busy with Henry and, from the window that looked over the farmyard, I could see Abel shoveling manure from the heap outside the cowshed into a wheelbarrow. I thought the coast was clear, but as soon as I was inside the little house, I heard Abel whistling. When I came out, he was spreading the muck on his mother's kitchen garden. I stuck my nose in the air and determined to ignore any rudeness, but he didn't tease, just looked up and smiled, very easy and friendly. He said, "How's the old squirrel, then?"

When Abel sang, it was like a bird singing; bright, sharp, and pure. Even speaking, his voice was lovely; a light, lilting, Welsh voice. His eyes were the same blue as his mother's; a clear summer blue, like pieces of sky. He said, "Mother says you'll be wanting the old cage out of the attic. Seems a pity to me, to be shutting a wild creature up. Still, I suppose it keeps you city folk busy. You've got the time for it. Not like us old farmers, nothing but work."

Abel wasn't all that keen on work! Under his father's eye, he kept at it. When he wasn't being watched, he skived off. He was leaning on his fork now. I said, "If you like, I'll do a bit of that for you."

I enjoyed spreading muck, digging the fork into the steaming pile and flinging it over the newly turned earth. And Abel was happy to watch me. He said, "You've got some good muscles for a girl, I'll say that."

I thought he meant I was fat. I jabbed the fork into the ground and said, "At least I'm not lazy like you."

"If I go a bit slower, it's because I have to keep on. I can't do like you, a bit here, a bit there, as the fancy takes me. Farming's a piece of fun for you. It's a life sentence for me."

He took the fork and sighed. I said, "If you hate farming, why don't you do something else?"

He shrugged his shoulders. "Dad wouldn't hear of it. Your mother's been on at my mother about my leaving school. Seems your mother reckons I ought to stay on after the summer. Dad won't hear of that either."

"Do you want to stay on at school?"

I couldn't think that he did. School was work, too. What Abel liked best was singing and riding. He rode the white pony round and round the chicken field; sometimes he stood upright on her bare back, knees loose and bendy, like a boy in a circus. I said, "Mum used to be a teacher, that's why she's so keen on education. But if you could choose what you wanted to do out of everything in the whole world, what would you want to do, *really*?"

I thought that I knew what I wanted. I loved the farm and all the things that I did; collecting eggs, walking with Mr. Jones down the Ten Acre to look at the young lambs, picking mushrooms and blackberries, helping with the harvest in summer. I even enjoyed mucking out the pigsty, though that may have been chiefly because Mr. Jones paid me a shilling to do it. Sometimes I thought I might marry Abel, but I kept this to myself because I didn't think he was likely to ask me. I didn't think anyone would ever marry me; I was too plain and ordinary.

I said, "I'd like to live in the country forever and ever."

"And I'd like to live in the city. Near a town, anyway. Seems we're both in the wrong box," Abel said. He started forking up the manure and hurling it around energetically. There were red lines on his forehead, on his fair skin, and his mouth had gone thin. Although I stayed on for a little while, he didn't seem to want to talk anymore. Abel was never bad tempered, he wasn't a quarrelsome person, but there was suddenly something angry about him.

Abel brought the cage up later that day and our mother put Henry in it. "Just an experiment, somewhere he'll be safe when we aren't around to look after him. There's the fire, and the oil stove. We'll just try for a minute. . . ."

"Don't be frightened, Henry," James said. "It's for your own good."

Henry wasn't frightened. He flew into a terrible rage! He splayed out his skinny legs and arms as he clung like a bat to the bars; he sprang from one side to the other, ears laid back, swearing. "*Vut, vut, vut.*" His button eyes blazed. "Sorry, Henry," our mother said, hastily unfastening the door. Henry ran up her arm and sat on her shoulder. Quite calm now, he washed himself and tidied his fur.

"Well!" our mother said. "What an exhibition!"

Abel doubled up laughing, slapping his hand on his corduroy breeches. "I'll take the old cage back," he said. "Seems there's one creature round here who means to be free to do what he pleases."

31

FOUR

Earlier that year, our mother had bottle-fed a lamb she called Rosy Posy. It had grown big enough now to be put with the flock, but every time Mr. Jones took it down the Ten Acre field, it ran away and came back to the yard, baaing under our window and calling for our mother.

"Rosy thinks she's a human," James said.

"Mr. Jones says there's more to sheep than most people reckon," I told him. "Only he says *ship*. There's more to ship than most people reckon."

"I wonder what Henry thinks," James said.

Whatever he thought, about us or about his new home, he knew what he wanted and was determined to tell us. He didn't want to be shut in a birdcage. He didn't want to sleep in a box of hay. That second night after supper we had a last game with him and took him to the box, expecting him to make a dash for his nest. But each time we put him in, he came out again and made for the chair where James had slung his jacket the night before. He didn't lose his temper; he was too tired. He just hopped backward and forward, little staggery, drunken hops, looking small and pathetic.

"All right, all *right*," James said, rolling his eyes up. "Don't mind me! I'm happy to freeze to death, long as you're comfortable!"

He took his jacket off and put it down on the chair. Henry shot into the sleeve, and after a bit of bumping about, that was that. He had settled himself for the night.

He slept there for about a week, asking to go to bed every evening at seven o'clock by jumping from side to side on the back of the chair. "Lucky the weather's turned so nice and warm, James," our mother said.

Then, one bedtime, Henry changed his mind. Charlie found him hopping into the linen basket in the kitchen. He took him back to the sitting room and pushed him up the sleeve of James's jacket. But Henry had given up the jacket, just as he had given up the hay box. He preferred the dirty washing in the linen basket. Charlie was as determined as Henry. He went on poking Henry into the jacket sleeve. Each time, Henry popped out again. "Give it up as a bad job, Charlie," our mother said.

"It's *blank* bad training to let him win," Charlie said. "If you'd trained *blank* Rosy better, if you didn't baa back at her, she might give up and decide to be a sheep for a change."

"Rosy thinks I'm her mother," our mother said. "I can't just ignore her. Sheep have their feelings. So do squirrels. If Henry wants to sleep with your dirty socks, then we'll have to let him."

I woke before James the next morning. Charlie was still asleep, too. Our mother said, "See if you can find Henry."

I looked in the linen basket. No Henry! But our mother was smiling, so I knew nothing dreadful had happened. She put her finger to her lips, and I spotted a bright eye peeping out of the pocket of her old gardening coat that hung on the back of the kitchen door. She whispered, "Don't let him know that you know. He thinks he's found somewhere private."

She was right. From then on, the coat pocket was Henry's secret. His favorite place for a nap in the daytime was on our mother's shoulder, curled up under her sweater like a little shoulder pad. But he always slept in the old coat at night and he would never go there if anyone was watching him, even if it meant being late for bed. If one of us was in the kitchen he would wait, washing his ears and his bottom, or sit on the top of the door with his arms folded across his white chest, pretending to have a quiet think. In the mornings, although his head would pop up out of the pocket the moment our mother went into the kitchen to light the oil stove and cook breakfast, he wouldn't move until she had turned her back on him. Then he would nip out and onto her shoulder, close up to her neck, chuckling away to himself, and scrabble about in her hair, scattering hairpins and unfastening her bun. When all her hair was loose, he would swing on it.

He liked to swing on the curtains, too, especially if the windows were open and there was enough breeze to stir them, hanging on by his legs, upside down, while he thrust his arms out in front and gave a long, lazy stretch. He seemed to like the wind. Sometimes he would sit on the windowsill, head up, nose quivering, rocking a little, his tail not curved over his back as it usually was, but spread out stiffly behind him, his tiny ears up and forward as if he were listening.

I liked to watch him, but James fretted. "We ought to keep the windows shut. He'll fall out."

And one day he did. He tumbled—or jumped, perhaps—into the chicken field. Charlie, playing down by the brook with the Morgan boys, saw him drop. He raced up the field, but by the time he was thundering up the stairs, breathing hard, sobbing, Henry

was already safe home. He had found his way round the house, in through the back, up the stairs. I had heard the tapping and skittering sound his feet made on the bare, polished oak boards, seen his dancing shadow in the bar of light under the door as he hopped backward and forward, asking to be let in. Our mother said, "You see? He isn't a pet or a prisoner! He's *chosen* to stay with us! He thinks we're his family."

Behind her back, James rolled his eyes at me. She was *potty*! How could anyone know what a squirrel was *thinking*? But she looked so pleased and so happy, we didn't say anything.

After that, we took him outdoors with us and let him run free. Spring was early that year, long, warm, blue days, and the cherry blossoms were out in the orchard. We put Henry down on the grass and he started picking the daisies. He held one in his hand and picked off the petals as if he were playing he-loves-me-he-loves-me-not. He ate what was left. Then he leapt for a cherry tree and ran up it, vanishing among the top branches. When we saw him again, he was sitting high above us, close to the sky, eating the blossom.

"Daysis," James wrote in his notebook, adding to the list of things Henry ate. "Chery blosom." James was amazingly clever at some things; he could draw trains and cars and any kind of machinery, getting the scale and the perspective right without measuring, just by looking; he could do complicated sums in his head in a flash and he understood logarithms. But he was a hopeless speller. He knew what a word should look like, he said, but the letters got scrambled up in his head.

"Henry," we called, that first day in the orchard. "Henry . . ."

He paid no attention, and we were anxious to start with; James scowled and sighed, and Charlie's face puckered. But although he never came when he was called, only when he thought he would, we soon found that he didn't like to leave us for long. He would dash down a tree, leap from shoulder to shoulder, and be off again. When we got bored, we only had to begin walking away and he would be with us at once, running round and round one of us, as he would run round the trunk of a tree. We carried him indoors like that, without touching him with our hands.

He loved to run free in the orchard, but if we took him farther afield, around the farm, or up to the little shop at the end of the lane, he was much less bold, never leaving whichever human tree he was using for transport. We got so used to carrying him about with us, in a pocket or tucked into a shirt, that sometimes when he was quiet, either asleep or just resting, we forgot he was there.

Mrs. Jones had a married daughter who lived in the next valley. She harnessed the trap and set off for a visit one morning and took Charlie and me and our mother along for the ride. Rosy chased our mother down the lane, baaing, but she stopped when she got to the brook. Rosy didn't like getting her feet wet, or crossing the wooden slats of the footbridge at the side of the water splash. "Silly *blank* Rosy," Charlie said. "Baa, baa, you silly sheep, we'll be back soon!"

The trap lurched a bit through the brook and up the rutted lane, but when we got to the metaled main road, Mrs. Jones clicked her tongue and we bowled along at a fair pace, the iron wheels of the trap humming, the harness creaking, the white pony throwing her head up and rattling the bit. She started to canter and Mrs. Jones had to tug hard on the reins to slow her down to a trot.

"Abel's been riding her too much," Mrs. Jones said. "Made her flighty. You ride a horse too much, it's spoiled for the trap. Not that I grudge Abel that bit of pleasure. He takes after my family when it comes to horses. They were the breath of life to my dad. It was his business of course, buying and selling, but it was more than money to him. He'd bred his own stable and he loved them like children. Riding horses, not workhorses. The day before he died, nigh on eighty, he'd been out on his chestnut stallion. Abel's got a lot of his grandfather in him. My brother's running the stables now, he's always said he'd take Abel on anytime, glad to have him. Abel would be glad to go, I daresay, only of course Mr. Jones says he can't spare him."

"Seems a pity if that's what he wants to do," our mother said. "If he's not keen on farming."

"Well, he's born to it, isn't he?" Mrs. Jones said. "Some people can't choose in this life. When I was young, I had a mind to go into the horse-dealing business, follow my dad. But he said, you help your mam, that's what girls do, and so that's what I did. Left school at fourteen, and waited on the men and worked round the house."

My mother raised her eyebrows. She thought this was wrong. She had taught James to sew on his own buttons and darn his own socks as well as doing his share of washing the dishes and carrying water. Girls should have the same chance as boys to do what they wanted, she always said, meaning the things *she* would have liked to do, like exploring Tibet to look for the yeti, or traveling alone into dangerous jungles to make friends with savage, wild animals—the sort of things that made me feel hollow inside just to think about. I didn't want to stay home and darn socks, but I could never, I thought, be as brave as my mother.

Nor could Mrs. Jones. Perhaps she wouldn't have been as frightened as I would have been if she came face to face with a tiger, but she was frightened of small, darting creatures like squirrels. When Henry peeped out of Charlie's pocket she let out a scream— not very loud, but sharp enough to startle the pony into a gallop. The trap jerked and quivered. Charlie hung on to his side, I hung on to mine, and our mother, sitting in the middle, hung on to both of us. Mrs. Jones stood up, thin legs braced, and hauled on the reins. She shouted, "Whoah, good girl! Whoah, Angel!"

We careered round a corner, the trap tilting sideways. Mrs. Jones's hat blew off and landed in my lap. Her black hair streamed out behind her. Although she looked frail, she was strong. She brought the pony to a halt, finally. It stood, restless and stamping and steaming. Devil would be a more suitable name than Angel, I thought. I jumped out of the trap and held its head, trying not to notice its fiery breath, its long yellow teeth, and the mad way its eyes rolled above me.

The trap was slewed across the road. Mrs. Jones was sitting down now. Her face was white and her mouth had gone blue. She said, "That creature! Nearly had us in the ditch!" She didn't mean the pony.

Charlie had pushed Henry down in his pocket. He kept his hand over him. He said, "I forgot that I'd got him. But he wouldn't have hurt you, Mrs. Jones, honest! He was asleep, and he just woke up, and wanted to see where he was."

"You know he makes Mrs. Jones nervous. You should be more careful," our mother said. But I could see that she thought it was a bit of a joke, all the same.

I said, "Not everyone fancies the idea of something quick and wriggly running up their legs. Mice, rats, squirrels, anything like that! Even Charlie makes a fuss sometimes!"

"Henry doesn't hurt," our mother said. "He doesn't even ladder your stockings. And squirrels are more intelligent than rats, anyway!"

She frowned, trying to understand how anyone could really object to Henry. "He's so light and so gentle! At home, he dashes about all over the place, among my ornaments, everywhere, and he never does any damage."

"You'll be telling me next that he's learning to talk," Mrs. Jones said, rather dryly.

"Oh, but he can talk," Charlie said. "He can swear!"

Mrs. Jones laughed. She gathered the reins and lifted the pony's head. As I got back into the trap she winked at me. "It sounds as if someone has been setting him a real bad example. And I don't mean our Bill!"

Charlie turned suddenly crimson. He sat quiet for the rest of the journey, his eyes dark and thoughtful.

It wasn't quite true that Henry never did any damage. He ate Charlie's kingfisher egg. (Well, of course, Charlie should never have taken it, but he hadn't seen a nest made of bones before.) He chewed James's slingshot. ("Getting a bit of his own back," our mother said.) And he stole James's pencils, not any old stub, but his very best, full-length drawing pencils, stripping every tiny splinter of wood and removing the long piece of lead, quite unbroken. He didn't eat the lead. It was just a good game to him. ("Poor little chap, he has to have something to play with," our mother said.)

He never harmed anything that *she* cared about, naturally! She had put her most precious things, a cut-glass scent bottle that our father had given her, and some small china figures that had belonged to her mother, out of Henry's reach on her dressing table. The table had three mirrors, one in the middle and two at the sides, and from the dining table Henry could see himself in them. He longed to get closer, but it was too long a leap for him. He didn't give up, though. He practiced regularly, dancing from side to side, his hops growing longer and stronger. The day we came back from visiting Mrs. Jones's married daughter, he finally managed it. He gathered himself for the spring, launched himself into the air, and landed beside the scent bottle.

Our mother gasped. But nothing was broken. And Henry made straight for a jug of bluebells that stood there and started eating them as fast as he could— not sitting on the edge of the jug, but on a bluebell stalk. The stalk bent a little with his weight for a second; then rose again, almost as upright as before. "Will you look at that!" said our mother.

It was a lovely, bright day. Outside the window, big, puffy, white clouds sailed across the blue sky, making moving shadow patterns on the bare, rounded hills. Clouds and sky were reflected in the three mirrors on the dressing table, and in front of them was Henry, balanced on a bluebell stalk.

"A fairy," our mother said, suddenly, softly. "A fairy creature. Isn't he, Charlie?"

Charlie blushed. He was too old for fairies. I thought he was going to swear, but he didn't. Instead, he smiled at our mother, his eyes round and dancing with mischief. "A *vut vut* fairy," he said.

FIVE

I had to go back to school. James and Charlie went to school in the market town three miles from the farm; James to the grammar school and Charlie to the primary. I could have gone to the same school as James, but the girls' school I had gone to in London had been evacuated to South Wales at the beginning of the war and our mother had decided that I would "do better" there. "Girls do better in single-sex schools," was what she said. "They need to work harder than boys if they are to get anywhere, and they have more of a chance if there aren't any boys to distract them." Perhaps she thought girls were more stupid than boys. Or that I was stupid. I didn't know and I didn't ask. I just did what I was told, as most children did then.

My school was in a mining town in a narrow valley where rows of terrace houses climbed steeply up the sides of the mountains and pointed slag heaps clustered around the pithead. During term time, I lived with a miner and his wife and their two grown-up sons who were both miners too, coming home off their shifts black-faced and white-eyed and smelling of coal dust; a nice, sharp, cindery smell. They were kind, and I liked them, as I quite liked my school, but after the farm it was all very dull to me; dull and gray, a kind of gray mizzle, or mist, over everything.

The war seemed much closer. On the farm we had an old battery wireless, but the batteries were always running down and so the news came to us very ghostly and faint, as if from another world a long way away. In the miner's house, the news blared out; bombings and battles, and, most important and frightening to me because of my father, attacks on convoys in the North Sea and the Atlantic; ships being sunk, blown out of the water. There was food rationing, too, which no one paid much attention to on the farm, where we could have butter and milk and fresh eggs for the asking. And in the town air-raid wardens were stricter about not showing lights after dark. In the country, although our mother was always careful to put up the blackout before we lit the oil lamps, you could usually see a yellow twinkle from another farmhouse across the valley or up on the mountain. Nights in the mining town were solidly dark, a heavy and breathless dark, so that when the stars came out and the moon rose, the lit night sky seemed to make the earth blacker.

Although I wasn't happy, I wasn't unhappy either. I got up in the morning, washed my face and brushed my teeth and ate breakfast and went to school. I came back in the afternoon and did my homework and ate supper and brushed my teeth and listened to the loud news on the wireless and went to bed. Other things did happen in term time, of course, but they don't really belong in this story, which was going on without me, in another part of Wales, in another valley. When I thought about myself in the mining town, I thought in black and white, but when I thought about the farm, I thought in bright colors; Bill's red hair, Abel's blue eyes. And I thought of Henry, sitting in front of the mirrors on our mother's dressing table; Henry eating bluebells and multiplied by three.

Our mother wrote to me twice a week. Charlie wrote a bit at the end of each of her letters. James didn't write, but once our mother sent a list he had made for me of all the things Henry had eaten. It was a very long list by now. It included a whole week's cheese ration for three people that Henry had stolen from the shelf in the kitchen. "He ate every scrap.

We should have called him Ben Gunn," our mother wrote.

She said James had forgotten to mention that Henry appeared to enjoy ink and Plasticine, and that although neither of these things was very nutritious, they hadn't done him much harm that she could see. And Charlie had given him toffees to tease him. Henry had a lot of trouble with the first toffee, as it stuck to his coat, to his chin and his feet, but he soon solved the problem. He had put the second toffee down, very carefully, and nibbled away without touching it. James had thought this so clever, he decided that it was time for Henry to be properly educated, so he took him to school the next day, tucked away in his pocket. Henry slept through morning assembly, through geography and geometry, waking up for French, a lesson that obviously excited him because he shot out of his sleeping place like a bullet the moment it started and bounded from desk to desk while the girls screamed and the boys tried to chase him and the teacher shouted to James to *do something about it,* which James couldn't do, since he was laughing so helplessly. James had expected to get into trouble, a hundred lines or a detention, but instead the teacher had said that if she had to have a wild animal like Henry rampaging round in her classroom she might as well see that they all got some benefit. So the whole class had to spend the next study period writing an essay about him.

Sometimes our mother sent me news about Dad, who sent us love in his letters, but didn't have time to write to each of us separately. He had had a few days' leave in America and had been to New York. He had seen the Empire State Building and the Statue of Liberty, and he said that New York was a beautiful city, full of tall towers called skyscrapers that really did seem to scrape the sky when you stood in the street and looked up at them soaring above you. But mostly she wrote about Henry; how intelligent he was, how clever, how funny. One day, when there was no fire in the grate, Henry had decided to explore up the chimney. He went up a red squirrel and came down a black one, every inch of him covered in soot. "You'll never guess what happened next!" she wrote. "He jumped onto the dining table and dived straight into a bowl of stewed rhubarb! He had quite a busy time cleaning himself up after that, I can tell you!"

Sometimes her letters made me smile; sometimes they made me feel homesick; sometimes they made me feel jealous. They seemed to be having so much fun. No one seemed to mind that I wasn't there. No one missed me. And by the time the summer holidays came, Henry would have forgotten me!

But Henry didn't forget. At the end of the term I went home. I went by train to Shrewsbury where I caught our local bus. The stop was about a mile from the farm and when I got off, Charlie and James were there. James had brought his bike to wheel my suitcase home and Charlie had brought Henry, sitting up on his shoulder. He was a lovely coppery color, he had spiky tufts in his ears, and his tail was fuller. I said, "Henry, you've grown!" and he jumped on me instantly. He ran all over me, circling me, as if he were saying, "I know this old tree!" Then he started smelling my face, working with his nose around my eyes and my ears and my mouth, giving a little lick here, a quick nibble there. His feet pads were soft and cold, like little cool, velvet cushions.

I laughed and laughed. I was so happy. Henry settled on my coat collar and started combing my hair. James took my suitcase and rested it on the bar of his bike. Charlie put his hand in mine, and I felt the calluses on his palm and his fingers and stroked them with my thumb. He gave a little skip and said, "I'm *glad* you've come home. Mum's made a special curranty cake, Dad sent some currants to us from America, and we've got a roast chicken and some of Mrs. Jones's peas for your coming-home supper."

James was wheeling his bike just ahead of us. He said, without turning round, "Dad sent nuts for Henry, too, a box of nuts wrapped up in waxed paper. Henry's first nuts, but he knew what they were before the parcel was opened, and he went absolutely mad, tear-

ing at it, scattering paper, until he got to the nuts and took one and ran away with it."

"We ate the rest," Charlie said. "We gave some to Mrs. Jones, but we had the most of them. Mum said they were too salty for Henry. It was silly of Dad to buy salted nuts. Mum says, salt isn't natural for squirrels."

"How should Dad know that?" James said indignantly, stopping his bike to wait for us to catch up with him. "Dad hasn't made a special study of squirrels the way we've all had to."

He looked at me now with a sudden, shy grin. James was always shy when we had been apart for a while, as if he was afraid that something might have happened to change things between us.

I said, "How's the list going? Henry's food list."

His grin became broader. "Mum's turning it into a spelling bee. She calls it improving the shining hour. She tells people she used to be a teacher but she's never stopped, really. Time she's finished with me, I'll be fit for a job as a cook. Or a grocer. I can spell just about everything you might think of as a bit of a tasty treat for your stomach. I should think nuts will be tops in the end, when they're ripe and ready, but up to now, porridge and mushrooms are pretty fair favorites."

"And *apples*," Charlie shouted, swinging so hard on my arm that I almost fell over. "Tell her about apples, James."

"That's not something to tell about, that's something to *see*! You keep quiet, Charlie. Mum wants to *show* her! It's a shame to spoil other people's surprises."

"*Vut, vut, vut,*" Charlie said. He let go my hand and ran on, jumping in and out of the ditch, keeping both feet together; strong, energetic jumps, as if he were on a pogo stick.

"Of course, it's still swearing," James said. "But Mum says, since no one can translate it except us, it doesn't matter so much."

"It only sounds better. He's swearing in just the same way he was swearing before. He never knew what the words he was saying really meant, did he? They were just *vut, vut, vut* to him."

"It isn't the same. Mum says swearing is using good words in a bad way. Like bloody. I mean you can say a bloody finger or a bloody handkerchief. That's all right."

"When Bill says *bloody,* he means it as swearing. Just like when Charlie says *vut.*"

James sighed. "But Charlie knows squirrels can't swear. Not like people. So copying a squirrel can't really be swearing. Don't let's quarrel about it."

"I'm not quarreling, dummy!" I had forgotten how much James hated to argue. He was near to tears now; trying to blink away the prickly damp in his eyes. I said, "I wish I didn't have to go away to school. I miss everything. Are there any other surprises? I don't mean about Henry. I mean, about people."

"I came top in maths and bottom in English, as usual, but that's not much of a surprise, I suppose. And Dad might get a bit of leave, long enough to come to the farm, sometime this autumn. But that's only *might*, so it doesn't count, really. Mrs. Davies over the Bent Hill is having a baby and Mum met Mr. Davies in the lane and he said that since they'd got the three boys, he was hoping for a young heifer this time. Mum said she managed to keep a straight face, but it was a bit of an effort. And Mr. Jones is getting an Italian prisoner to help him. And we'll be starting to cut the wheat in the bottom field any minute; we're just waiting on Farmer Howard up at the Roveries to finish with the threshing machine. That's about all, I think. 'Cept for one thing. A real surprise about Abel." He glanced sideways at me, grinning a bit, but more slyly than shyly now.

"Tell me."

He shook his head, screwing his face up into creases. It made him look like a monkey.

I said, "Ape Face."

"If you call me rude names I won't tell you anything."

"Oh, I do beg your pardon. James the Wonderful, Noble Meeter of Sisters, Grand Suitcase Carrier, Chief News Bringer. Is that good enough?"

"Daft! All right, then. Abel's Uncle Josh came

to ask if Abel would like to work in his stables. Mr. Jones doesn't need him so much now he's got this Italian coming to help him, as well as old Bill. Abel thought, no chance, no point in even asking his father, but Uncle Josh talked to Mrs. Jones and she talked to Mum, and they each had a go at Mr. Jones and managed to persuade him between them."

I wasn't sure if I was more hurt than furious, or more furious than hurt. I said, "It's not fair! No one tells me anything. I'm packed off out of the way, *banished*, sent into *exile* like criminals were sent off to Australia years ago, and no one bothers to send me real news from home. *You* don't bother, do you? Mum writes about Henry, that's okay, I mean I like to hear about Henry, but it's not the only thing I'm interested in. She must think I'm some kind of *moron*."

"She tries to think of things to cheer you up and make you laugh," James said reproachfully. "She spends *ages* writing you letters, just as long as she spends writing to Dad, and he's her husband and he's fighting the war. And she couldn't have written about Abel, anyway, because we didn't know till last night. Mrs. Jones came up with the chicken for your coming-home supper and asked Mum to have a word with Mr. Jones. She said Mr. Jones has got a lot of time for Mum's opinion. Mum was down there for hours."

I thought of Mr. Jones, who was a quiet man, a bit stooped over and tired looking. If Mrs. Jones didn't

55

light the lamp in the evening, if she were out or busy in the dairy, he wouldn't bother; he would sit in the dark on the oak settle in the big kitchen and stare into the glowing range fire. Sometimes he would suck the ends of his long, drooping moustache and sigh, but mostly he just sat, very still, very silent. Perhaps he was silent because Mrs. Jones was such a good talker, or perhaps she talked so much because he talked so little. But whichever way round it was, I felt sorry for him. He didn't stand much of a chance against Mrs. Jones and none at all against Mrs. Jones and my mother together. On the other hand, I was glad for Abel's sake that they had won. Though a bit sad for mine.

I said, "When's he going? I mean, it's all right for *you.* You're here all the time! But it's rotten for me if everyone goes away as soon as I come home for the holidays!"

"*I'm* not going anywhere," James said gently. He gave me one of his pained looks and I knew why. We were both jealous about Abel. But we were jealous about each other, too.

Mixed-up feelings like that bothered James more than me, so I said, "Of course, I'd rather have you, if I had to choose," and although I felt guilty as soon as I'd said this because it sounded as if I didn't care about Abel, it made James feel better.

He said, much more cheerfully, "He won't be

going until the harvest is in, anyway. That's what Mum said last night. She was thinking you might be upset. She worries how you feel about going away while Charlie and I stay at home, so it's mean to talk about being sent off to Australia as if she was trying to get rid of you. Australia's a lot farther away than South Wales."

James always took what you said very seriously. It was hopeless trying to explain that you hadn't meant quite what you'd said, not those exact words. He would only want to know why, in that case, you had said them.

I might have tried, all the same, but we were nearly home now. I could see the triangle of grass and the white rail that marked the end of our lane and, through a gap in the hedge, the farmhouse itself, lower down in the valley, but standing on a little rise so that the ground fell away all around it, leaving it standing proud, a big plain white house with tall chimneys and a corner of the barn showing beyond it. I didn't want to talk any longer. I felt too shivery and excited.

And James knew how I felt. He said, "You run on if you want. I can manage the case and the bike." I looked at him to make sure and saw he was smiling a smoothed-out, happy smile and knew that he was over his shyness and we were friends again.

S I X

Abel was over the moon. He got up the same time as Bill in the mornings and sang like a lark; a happy sound, full-throated and bubbling. The well had run low in the dry summer heat and only a trickle of brackish, brown water with wriggly things in it came out of the pump. Abel took the trap and filled churns at the brook twice a day, enough for the whole house. He groomed the white pony and the two big, heavy cart horses; plaited their manes and their tails and brushed their coats glossy. He worked in the harvest field harder than anyone; even the Italian prisoner, who was older and stronger, couldn't keep up with him.

A lot of farmers had prisoners of war living with them. People said the Germans were the best workers, but the Italians were more popular with the farmers' wives because they were so ready to help round the house—carry buckets, chop wood, and mend bicycles. "The sort of things their own husbands and sons don't do for them," our mother said.

Our Italian prisoner was called Mario Angelo Benati. He was quite old, about thirty, with gray in his curly black hair and a tanned, shriveled face. I was a bit disappointed because he wasn't as romantic-looking as I'd expected, but he smiled a lot and was very friendly. He liked to show photographs of his family back home in Naples—his mother, his wife, and his little boy, who was called Achilles. Mario's son was about Charlie's age, a fat boy with big, solemn, dark eyes. Charlie was fascinated by him and was always asking to be shown his picture. "Tell me about your boy, Mario. Is he as strong as I am? Can he ride a bike? Can he climb trees good as me?"

Mario couldn't speak much English and Charlie couldn't speak Italian, but they seemed to understand each other. Charlie trailed around after Mario, chattering away, and Mario answered him, always patient and smiling. James had given Charlie his slingshot, the one Henry had chewed leaving teeth marks all over it, and Mario made Charlie a new one of elm wood, beautifully polished with engine oil. "I wish Mario was my dad," Charlie said when he showed it to me.

I felt sorry for our father who was so far away,

but I was even sorrier for Bill, who was here, and clumping off to fetch the cows on his own. James said that he was probably glad not to have Charlie hanging round his neck all the time, and although there was no way of knowing how Bill really felt, since it was as hard to have a proper conversation with him as it was with Mario, I thought I had better do something to make up for Charlie. I helped with the milking; stripping the cows after they had been on the milking machine and, in spite of being nervous in case one of them kicked me, I began to enjoy the warm manure smell, the wet chomping noise the cows made when they ate, and the sound of the milk jetting into the pails; a growly sound when the pail was empty and a soft, liquid *swish* as it filled. Bill didn't talk much, he didn't even swear very much while I was around, but once he said, "You'm a right smart little maid," and let out a huge guffaw that set the cows shifting and stamping.

I took Henry milking one evening and he sat on the edge of the pail, quite still for a while, watching the hissing streams of white milk. Then he decided to investigate further. He leaned forward too far and fell in. When I fished him out he looked very comic, with all his hair plastered down. I thought he would never be able to clean himself properly and the milk would make his fur stiff as it dried, so I took him indoors and bathed him in a bowl of warm water. I wrapped him in a towel afterward, but he still looked very damp and bedraggled when I let him go. He shot off my lap, landed on our mother's bed, and dived under the quilt. There was nothing to be seen after that for quite a long time except for a series of little bumps undulating rapidly up and down the quilt, like a snake in a hurry.

When he came out he was dry, but he still wasn't satisfied. He went in for a long cleaning session, paying particular attention to the backs of his ears, supporting one arm with the other so that I could see the insides of his hands as he nibbled away at them, and ended by sweeping his tail through his fingers. Then he spread his legs wide and slid on his tummy up and down the back of a chair to clean under his chin. All this made him tired, and since it was washday and the fire was lit to air clothes, he sat on the hearth rug in front of it. He stared into the fire and, very slowly, his head nodded lower and lower, until he was lying face down on the rug, his small, tufted ears flat on the floor in front of him.

"You must have worn him out," James said, coming in with our mother, each of them lugging a billowing basket of washing. "He only sleeps on his front like that when he's really exhausted."

"He looks like a Moslem, praying in the mosque," our mother said. "As if he had heard the muezzin calling the faithful to prayer."

61

I told them he had fallen into the milk pail, but I didn't tell them how cleverly he had dried himself. They had had Henry to themselves for so long, it was my turn to have a secret. I said, "Perhaps when he wakes up, we could give him an apple."

Until now, I had forgotten what Charlie had said about apples. There had been so much that was new. Hazelnuts, for one thing. Henry loved them, and I loved watching him, holding a bunch in his long, flexible fingers and nipping off the end of the nut, very neatly, making no mess, to get at the kernel. We all gathered them for him; even Bill sometimes came back from fetching the cows with his greasy old cap brimming full. And Henry was clever. He never opened a nut that was bad; he could tell by the weight. And he always knew when one of us had been out collecting. James usually had a few on him and Henry had only to jump on his head to know where they were. No sniffing around from pocket to pocket; one second there was a boy and a squirrel, the next just a boy. If you were quick you might spot a flash of red, a movement somewhere in James's jacket, but that was all.

He wasn't supposed to be on the table at mealtimes. "Not allowed," our mother would say. "A-ah! Naughty!" He knew what that meant! He liked cleaning up the remains of the porridge bowl and if she told him off, he would tighten his toes on the edge of the bowl and swear at her dreadfully. He swore at the spoon in the porridge bowl, too, because it got in his way. At first, he just pushed it aside with his nose and got very annoyed when it kept slipping back. He would push it away over and over again, faster and faster, making a fearful clatter, his voice rising angrily. *Vut, vut.* At last, one day, he found the solution; he picked the spoon up in his mouth and pitched it out of the bowl. Then he looked at us, very pleased with himself, as if waiting for the applause.

Nuts were his favorite food, but he liked porridge, and sweets, and cheese, and raisins, and prune stones, and cake. Anything he couldn't quite finish he put aside for a rainy day, filling little holes in our old armchairs and in the pleats at the top of the window curtains. When our mother drew the curtains at night to hide the ugly old blackout frames, she was showered with whatever Henry had put by that day. He even tried to hide things down the backs of our necks, jumping on our shoulders and poking bits of toast and pieces of fruit inside our shirts. Once he tucked a half-chewed and very sticky Pontefract cake inside James's ear.

I knew Henry liked apples, but I had never seen him tackle a whole one. That evening, when he woke up from his nap on the hearth rug, our mother gave him a shining red Beauty of Bath almost as big as he was and certainly heavier. Henry fell upon it as if he were starving. But he didn't eat it. He went to work

with his teeth and his talons and sent chunks of juicy white apple flying around him. When he got to the core he sat down and looked at us in the same way as when he had got rid of the spoon from the porridge bowl. "How clever I am," he seemed to be saying. Then he removed the pips from the core, one by one. Then he peeled the pips!

"There!" our mother said proudly. "Isn't that something special to see? My word, some people are fussy about their food, aren't they? Of course, he's lucky to have the chance. In the wild, he'd have been hungry this summer. Summer is a lean time for squirrels, before the nuts come."

"Perhaps he'd rather be wild," James said. "He'd have other squirrels to play with."

"He's got us," Charlie said indignantly. "He's got four extra good trees. Not just nut trees but trees that grow biscuits and sweets and all sorts of nice things. I bet he's glad he hasn't got to find his own food."

"He can't be *glad*," James said. "I mean, he can't be glad because he's never had to look after himself, so he doesn't know if he'd like it better or not. He only knows what it's like to be a pet. He might rather be a real squirrel."

He was looking solemn. Our mother said, "You don't think he's unhappy with us, do you, James?"

" 'Course he's not!" Charlie's face flamed red as fire.

"I know that," James said. "It's just . . ." He

seemed to be struggling; as if there was something he thought that he ought to say but didn't really want to say or didn't know how to.

Our mother was watching him with an odd, sad expression. "Do you think that we ought to set him free now he's grown? Is that what you mean, James?"

"I don't know. No, of course I don't want to. That's not *it*, though. I mean, what *I* want. He might not know how to find his own food. He might starve and die."

"He'd have to take that chance, wouldn't he? He might find a mate and start his own family."

"We're his family," Charlie roared. He jumped up and down with rage. "And he's my squirrel, I found him, I brought him home! And he *wants* to stay with us, he's been off on his own loads of times and he always comes back. . . ." He started to cry, mouth open, bawling.

Our mother scooped Charlie up and sat down, holding him tight on her lap, rocking him. "Hush," she said. "Hush." Over his heaving shoulder she shook her head at James. "Charlie's right, you know. We haven't exactly forced Henry to stay. We haven't kept him a prisoner."

"I was just *thinking*," James said in a hurt voice.

Charlie twisted around. He was so soggy with tears that his nose ran as well as his eyes and his mouth. "I'd *die* if he went. I want him to stay with us forever and ever. . . ."

SEVEN

I didn't see any wild squirrels that summer. Perhaps Henry's parents had taken off somewhere safer after Charlie had shot their nest down with the slingshot. Red squirrels like conifer forests, our mother said, and although tall trees grew along the lanes in the thick, heavy hedgerows, there were no real deep woods in the valley; the patchwork of fields flowed up the sides of the hills to the stony, green, sheep-cropped uplands and the heathery summits.

I saw a stuffed squirrel, though. Our postman had a small holding, a couple of cornfields at the back of his cottage a mile up our lane, and one week I did his round for him while he got his harvest in. Abel saddled up the white pony for me. She was in foal and much quieter; riding her now was like riding a slow-moving barrel. I delivered the mail and collected it, too; I had a hanging scale with a hook on it for weighing parcels so that I could charge the right money. It was a good job; the postman paid me fifteen shillings, and, although I was scared of farm dogs even when they were chained, I felt fairly safe on the pony.

Farthingale's Farm was at the bottom of a steep gully, what Welsh people call a *cwm*, a narrow cleft in the mountain. The path was too steep to ride Angel down, so I tethered her at the top and went down the cwm a little way to listen for dogs. I could tell from the envelopes that it was only a couple of bills that I had to deliver, and if I'd heard barking I would have done what the postman had told me to do: put them under a stone until the next time. "No point in taking trouble over the bills," he had said. "Farmers don't pay until they gets the red warning."

But there was no sound this hot, windless morning except a drowsy bee humming somewhere.

I wondered if the house was empty. The ground-floor windows were shuttered and a dusty curtain of ivy trailed over the door, which didn't have a knocker or a letter box. There was no sign of life in the yard; no ducks, no chickens, no geese, no horse in the stable, no pig in the sty. I thought that I would have to put the bills under a stone after all. Then, suddenly, the door opened and there was a rush of cold air, like damp breath. I looked into the hall—and turned dizzy with terror.

An enormous dog stood there; a brindle hound with glittering eyes and a red mouth, open and snarling.

It was like the very worst nightmare. My ears sang, I tried to scream but no sound came out and I couldn't move, either; my legs were frozen solid, cold and heavy as stone. I heard a voice that seemed to come from a long way away. "Must be the sun."

Then I was sitting on a wooden settle, its straight back behind me. I was inside the house, in the dark hall. Between me and the open door that framed the bright day stood the terrible hound! It was motionless, its heavy hindquarters toward me, but any moment it would turn, leap, tear me to pieces! I shrank back and gasped. I managed to speak, though my tongue felt furry and swollen. I moaned, "Oh, the dog!"

Someone laughed. "That's only old Hero, girl. Long past doing you harm."

The dog was dead. A stuffed dog. There were moth holes in its brindled sides; the red mouth was painted; the glittering eyes made of glass.

Two little old men looked down at me anxiously. They were exactly alike; both bald as eggs with fat, bright cheeks like red blobs painted on, and they both wore thick-lensed, horn-rimmed spectacles. They weren't dressed like farmers. Their gray flannel trousers were scruffy but they were scruffy-indoors, not scruffy-outdoors, and the badges on the breast pocket of their blazers made them look like ancient schoolboys. I said, "I'm sorry I was so stupid."

They shook their heads, chuckling in unison. One twin said, "No call to apologize, little lady. Father made a good job of old Hero." And the other, "Nasty tempered in life, so he fixed him nasty tempered in death. We're used to him, but perhaps we should put him with the rest of Father's collection where he won't startle visitors. Is that why you've come? To see the collection? You show her, Sidney, while I fetch some refreshment. Help her to get over her fright."

He disappeared down the hall. Sidney beamed. "Saul has gone to fetch you a glass of cider. I'll do the honors."

He opened a door. The room beyond was dusky, but enough light slanted in through the top of the closed shutters to see the stuffed animals. They were all posed in lifelike positions. A fox crouched back on its haunches with one paw raised. A badger was hunting, its nose to the ground. A big group of stoats and weasels appeared to be playing together. Crows perched on a bit of dead tree, some hunched and roosting, some with spread wings. There were rabbits, and a hare, sitting up. Sidney said, "Father was a zoologist but he was an artist, too, on the side."

He sounded proud. I wondered how well he could see through those heavy glasses. All these animals had been dead a very long time. A film of dust covered them, their coats and feathers were spiky and dull, and most of them oozed little trickles of sawdust. In the corner of the room something small scuttered and scurried; a mouse, or several mice, taking cover. Sidney said, "Father used to say that if all the creatures were to vanish from the face of the earth, there would be his collection left for people to look at and marvel."

I couldn't think what to say. But he was waiting for me to say something. I said, "Do you have many visitors?"

He smiled, and the blobs of his cheekbones grew fatter. "I'll tell you a secret," he said. "You are the only one we have ever had, little lady. So take your time, look around at your leisure. Ah, there you are, Saul! Nectar from our own apples for our very first visitor."

The cider was cold and sour but the coldness and sourness stung my nose and took off the musty smell of the room. I sipped slowly as I inspected the animals, trying to look bright and interested and wondering how soon I could say thank you and go.

Then I saw the red squirrel. It was sitting on its haunches, its scraggy and moth-eaten tail curled over its back. Its arms were wired up in front and its hands closed together, but if it had been holding a nut between them, a mouse had stolen it long ago. And it had only one button eye.

I was glad that I hadn't brought Henry with me. It would have been a frightening thing for him to have seen—as frightening, I suddenly realized, as it would have been for me if I had come across a stuffed human in that horrible room. The stuffed squirrel was just a dead animal like all the others but for some reason it made me feel as strange and fluttery as if it had been a stuffed girl.

I finished the cider. I said thank you and goodbye politely. When I had climbed to the top of the path I turned and waved at Sidney and Saul who were standing outside the door, each with an arm raised in a stiff salute. It was the end of the week; the last day that I would do the mail round. I returned the bags and the weighing machine to the postman and was paid my wages. And then, jogging home on the pony, remembered that the bills I had gone to deliver to Farthingale's Farm were still in my pocket.

"A bit soft in the head, them old Farthingales," Abel said. "A right pair of dafties. Never go out, no one goes there. Never heard that their dad was anything special. Just an old gamekeeper, far as I know."

"I was lucky to get out alive," I said. "They might have caught me and stuffed me! Kept me in the hall with that horrible dog!"

James giggled. "Bet you were scared of that, weren't you?"

"Only a bit. Just to start with."

"Natural for girls to be a bit scared," Abel said kindly. "Girls are more tender than boys."

"She's more than ordinary scared," James said scornfully. "She'd be scared of a rabbit if it pulled a face at her!"

He was showing off in front of Abel. We were in the loft over the cowshed. There was a stall at the end where the bull was kept when it wasn't out in the field, and a trapdoor above the stall so that hay could be forked down into the manger. The bull was in the stall now and Abel had been feeding it. We looked down, through the open trap, at its broad back, its heavy, horned head.

"Mum says she doesn't know where she gets it from," James went on. "She won't even go into the *field* when the bull's there! She'd faint if it just took a *look* at her!"

"Shut up," I said. "Who's *she*? The cat's mother?"

James rolled about on the loft floor, pretending to be helpless with laughter. "She'd be scared of a mouse," he gasped, "she'd be scared of a *worm*. Bet you she'd even be scared of a *dead* worm. . . ."

"I'll kill you," I said. "If you don't stop, I'll push you down the trap to the bull and he'll kill you, tear your stomach out with his horns, and I shan't care, I'll just *laugh*."

"Oh, give over, the pair of you," Abel said. "That ole bull's safe as houses. Watch now, I'll show you."

He lay on his stomach and wriggled backward until his legs were dangling down through the trap. Below, the bull chewed the hay wetly and noisily. Abel whispered. "Keep quiet now, don't rile him." He lowered himself slowly and carefully. The bull went on, steadily munching. Abel sucked in his breath and dropped, hanging on with his hands. For a split second he was on the bull's back, legs astride; then he heaved himself up, scarlet in the face, grinning. The bull shifted restlessly. One horn crashed the wooden partition.

I said, "You wouldn't do that, would you, James? I'll show you who's scared."

I was too angry to be frightened; angry with James, angry with myself. As I lay on my stomach, and swung my legs down, I knew it would be harder for me than for Abel, who was taller and stronger than I was, but I wasn't afraid, even then. I dropped as Abel had done, keeping a grip on the side of the trap, and found that the bull's back was wider than I'd expected, and warmer; I could feel the hot muscles of its great neck rippling beneath me. I tried to spring up at once, but in that same moment the bull jerked its head down and I began to slip forward. I was scared then, all right! I heard Abel shout something, and felt my wrists seized as the bull raised its head again, but it was Mario who lifted me and dragged me clear of the horns, yanking me upward so sharply that I thought my arms would come out of their sockets. Safe in the loft, I started to giggle. Mario kicked the trap shut and glared at me fiercely.

"No laugh," he said. "Is great danger. *Perìcolo. Perìcolo di morte*. I tell. I tell the Mama."

When he had gone, Abel and James clung to each other, hooting with laughter, partly because they had been badly frightened, and partly because Mario had sounded so funny. I began to laugh with them. My wrists hurt, my shoulders burned, I might have been killed, but I felt wonderful; so proud and so happy. I had ridden on the back of a bull and no one could call me a coward any longer.

E I G H T

Our mother said, "Once in the lion's den is enough for any Daniel. Just remember that, will you?" But she sounded approving. Perhaps she was thinking that I might at last be growing into the sort of brave daughter she hoped for; a girl who might become a famous naturalist, or an elephant trainer.

Or perhaps she wasn't really thinking about me at all. She hadn't heard from our father for several weeks and although she said, "No news is good news," she sighed as she said it, and her face sagged a bit at the edges.

She was ironing, putting the heavy flatiron to heat on the oil stove until it sizzled when she spat on it, and hanging the things on the clotheshorse to air as she finished them. I was curled up in the old armchair reading *Wuthering Heights*. It was peaceful and pleasant; the *thump* of the iron, the nice, scorchy smell. James and Charlie were out. Henry was dozing on top of the tall bureau bookcase.

Or he had been dozing. He flashed over me suddenly, bounding from the back of the chair to the clotheshorse. He seized a sock in his mouth, leapt from the clotheshorse to the chair, from the chair to the curtain. He ran up the curtain, jumped to the top of a picture, and then to the top of the bookcase, which was about a foot from the ceiling. He left the sock there and was down again in an instant, snatching a handkerchief from the horse and tearing up again to add it to the sock. Up and down, up and down, over and over again, without pausing, adding table napkins, tea towels, more socks and handkerchieves, Charlie's underpants, a pair of my knickers.

We watched, amazed. One minute all had been order and quiet; the next, one small squirrel had removed all our clean washing to the top of the bookcase. I said, "He's gone bonkers."

Our mother was laughing. "He's just decided to make his own domestic arrangements. I wonder what put it into his head all of a sudden!"

I thought that she wouldn't have laughed like that if one of us children had scrumpled up all her

fresh ironing! But I was glad to see her look happy again; all the sad pouches had gone from the sides of her mouth.

She said, "I think he's finished his scavenging for the moment. Look at him now."

Henry wasn't visible, in fact, but tremendous heavings and bumpings were going on inside what was now a huge mound of washing as he set about rearranging his nest. A sock slipped out of bounds and was jerked back into place. And a bra. I said, "That's one of mine and I need it! All my others have got a bit small." I hadn't mentioned this before. I was the only girl in my class who was fat enough in the chest for a bra, and I was embarrassed about it.

She said, "Why didn't you tell me? We ought to go shopping. You need a bra, and James needs at least a couple of shirts, and Charlie needs just about everything. Oh, dear! I hope we've got enough clothing coupons."

She was looking worried again. I said quickly, "It doesn't matter. I can take it out of Henry's nest. If he is Henry. I mean, if he's making a nest, he could be Henrietta."

"Male squirrels make nests, too. A male's nest is called a buck's drey. Though I don't suppose they normally use people's underwear! Our clever Henry is just adapting himself to his circumstances."

I said, "If he was free, if we let him go, he wouldn't know what to do, would he? He wouldn't

80

find knickers and socks hanging about on the trees."

"I daresay he'd manage." She looked at me thoughtfully. She said, with a sudden sigh, almost a little groan, "Or he might not, of course. It's hard to know what to do for the best. I know James thinks we should let him go. But it would break Charlie's heart."

I felt a bit cross. Why was Charlie so special? I said, "James only half thinks that. I mean, he half thinks it for Henry. What's the best thing for *him*? But it's all kind of muddled up with what we feel as well." I thought about the stuffed squirrel at Farthingale's Farm. I said, "I mean, Henry's not just a creature to us, not just a pet animal, he's more of a *person*."

She sighed again, but it was a relieved sigh this time. She said, in her brisk teacher's voice, "Useful for your education, too. Not many children are lucky enough to have a natural history lesson in their own homes all day and every day. Henry's eating habits have even improved James's spelling! Now we've all got a chance to find out what a really resourceful young squirrel will do when he wants to make a nest and his father and mother aren't around to advise him."

After that day, nothing was safe anymore. Henry's nest making took up a great deal of his time and anything soft that he thought might be useful was likely to vanish. He even tried to drag heavy sweaters up to the top of the bookcase. He would go backward up the curtain pulling the sweater after him, using a ramming movement, first one hand, then the other, to push more and more of it into his tiny mouth. But a sweater was just a bit too cumbersome for him. Although he often got as far as the curtain top, he was always defeated by the double leap from the curtain to the picture, and from the picture to his nest. "Poor Henry, he tries so hard. I wish he could make it, just once," our mother said fondly.

We let him keep all the things we could spare and blamed him when we couldn't find something. "I expect Henry's got it," we said. It saved having to look.

We wore odd socks most of the time. Henry only ever took one of a pair. And Charlie lost more clothes than the rest of us because he left them lying about when he took them off. "Teach you to be tidier," our mother told him, but James said to me, privately, that he didn't think learning to put everything you thought you might want to wear again under a brick or a pile of books was all that useful a lesson.

The nest got bigger and bigger. It wasn't only clothes that disappeared. Henry liked paper—wrapping paper, paper bags, newspaper. The two bills for Farthingale's Farm that I had put behind the clock on the mantelpiece, meaning to give them to the postman sometime, were added to Henry's collection, and when at last letters arrived from our father, six of them on the same morning, Henry whipped them off the table before our mother had a chance to sit down and read them. He chattered angrily at her when she rummaged in his precious nest. "Sorry Henry," she apologized. "I really do beg your pardon."

After supper that evening, Mrs. Jones came to visit. It was quite late, around ten; Charlie was asleep in the bed in the corner, and James was sitting at the table with pencils and a big piece of paper, making a drawing of a combine harvester.

It had turned chilly. Our mother put a match to the fire and Mrs. Jones held out her pale hands to the warmth. She had got even thinner just lately and her fingers were almost transparent; I could see the flames through them. For once she wasn't talking much, just sitting quietly and listening while our mother read out bits of news that might interest her from our father's letters. His ship had been in a collision and was being repaired in a dry dock in Baltimore. Everyone in America was very hospitable, so he wasn't too lonely, but he missed us all very much, all the same. He had a special present for Charlie, something the ship's carpenter had made when he heard about the three holes in the privy and the paper blowing up through them, and he would try and find someone to deliver it to us, because although he had hoped to get home leave in the autumn, it seemed now that he was unlikely to be at the farm much before Christmas. He was looking forward to seeing us then, and to meeting Mrs. Jones and her family.

Mrs. Jones gave a little, dry laugh. "I hope I'm still here," she said, and I wondered what she meant, where she was going. But I was too deep in my book to pay much attention, and after that our mother started on the boring subject of clothes rationing, which was such a problem when you had fast-growing children, and I was even less interested. Their voices murmured on, gently rising and falling, and became a soothing background sound, like soft music. But I must have been listening with part of my mind. When Mrs. Jones said, "Do you think I'll have to give coupons for my shroud?" I looked up from my book.

Mrs. Jones had spoken in such a cheerful, practical voice that I thought I must have misheard her. I looked at James, but he was deaf to the world when he was drawing. I caught our mother's eye and she said, "Go and get the tea things out of the kitchen, there's a good girl. And don't disturb Henry."

N I N E

Our mother said, "Oh, she didn't mean anything. You know Mrs. Jones, how she runs on! I didn't know you were eavesdropping."

"I wasn't. You weren't talking privately. James and I were there, in the room. I just heard what she *said*. And I know what a shroud is. Is Mrs. Jones dying?"

"In a manner of speaking, I suppose we all are!"

But she knew that wasn't an answer. She gave me a measuring look; considering how much, or how little, to tell me. When she drew in her breath and lifted her chin, I knew she had made up her mind to be straight with me. "You know she's been ill. Well, she's not getting better. That's all anyone can really say, but Mrs. Jones is the sort of person who would rather face up to something than pretend it may never happen. That doesn't mean she'd want everyone to know. She doesn't want Mr. Jones to know, for one thing. Not yet, anyway. She wants to get Abel settled first. So don't you go around chattering. You know what you are!" I pulled a face and she added, more kindly, "And don't brood! Mrs. Jones wouldn't want you to be worrying, either!"

I could have told her that I wasn't worrying, or not in an unhappy way. I had never known anyone who thought she was going to die before and, although I was sorry, it was quite interesting and exciting to wonder how Mrs. Jones felt about it. But I knew that grown people didn't like it when you were honest about your real thoughts and feelings. I said, "I can't help being worried for Abel. I mean, it's awful for him, she's his mother!"

And then, at once, I was terrified. I said, "If it was *you*, I just couldn't bear it! You're all right, aren't you?"

She laughed, her eyes suddenly bright. She gave me a hug. "Silly girl. I'm strong as a horse! Good heavens, I haven't got time to be ill, with the four of you to look after!"

Four of us? I said, "Oh, you mean *Dad*! He's old enough to look after himself."

She went a bit pink. "Goose!" she said. And I knew she had really been thinking of Henry.

Our mother could be sharp sometimes, but she was always gentle when you were ill. If you weren't a little boy, or a baby squirrel, being sick was about the only sure way to get her full attention, and if James and I hadn't been so happy and busy that summer, we might have got headaches or stomach pains fairly frequently.

"Charlie first, Henry second, Mrs. Jones third," James said. "What's wrong with Mrs. Jones?"

It was toward the end of August. The harvest was nearly over; the last field almost cut. Abel and Bill were chasing the rabbits out of the remaining small square of standing corn, Charlie shrieking with excitement and horror whenever they managed to kill one with a stick. Mrs. Jones and our mother had brought jugs of cider and a basket of sandwiches and were setting them down in the shade of the hedge.

Mario was helping them. Except for my mother and me, he was the only person on the farm who seemed to know about Mrs. Jones. His laughing face was solemn when he looked at her, and he had been quick when she came through the gate to run and take the things she was carrying from her. Now both

he and our mother were fussing around her, finding the most comfortable place for her to sit, and making a kind of chair out of wheat sheaves.

I said, "How d'you mean, *wrong?*" I tried to look puzzled.

James looked at me and said nothing. He always knew when I was pretending.

I said, "We're not supposed to know. She's ill and she's not getting better. But she wants it kept secret. She doesn't want Mr. Jones to know until Abel is settled, is what she told Mum. I suppose she thinks Mr. Jones would tell Abel and she doesn't want Abel to worry about her when he goes off to work for his uncle."

"Oh, you are stupid!" James said.

"I am *not!* It's like Mum not writing to tell me when you and Charlie had measles so badly last year. There was nothing I could do to help and she didn't want me to worry."

James said, "It's nothing to do with anyone *worrying.* Mr. Jones doesn't want to let Abel go. If Mrs. Jones dies, he *won't* let him! She knows that. Abel knows it. Everyone knows it. Why don't you know it?"

Because no one told me, was the answer, of course, but James didn't stop to hear it. His face swelled up, dark as a ripe plum, and he ran off to chase rabbits. He hated to see anything killed, but he waved his arms and shouted louder than Charlie.

Mr. Jones was sitting on the shaft of the wagon with a pile of dead rabbits in front of him, picking them up one by one, making a slit in a hind leg and poking the other leg through it. Several rabbits were already hanging on the pole that was fixed along the side of the wagon. Thick blood dripped slowly from their mouths and there was dust on their eyes. I said, "Do you want any help, Mr. Jones?" and was glad when he shook his head.

I perched on the wagon shaft next to him. He shifted to make a little more room for me and I settled more comfortably. Mr. Jones rarely said much, he was a restful person to be with in that way, but it seemed unsociable to sit for too long saying nothing. I said, "I like working on the farm. I wish I could be a Land Girl instead of going back to school."

He gave a bit of a grunt. "Don't think your mam would think much of that. Schooling's a fine thing for a young lady."

This was quite a long speech for Mr. Jones. I said, "Mum wants me to stay on and take all sorts of boring exams and go to university, but I think it's more important to do something for the war effort, really. And I like working hard, and I don't mind what I do. I mean, I'd like to learn how to plow and to harrow, but I can look after chickens and work in the dairy and clean out the pigs and help dip the sheep. I know I'm not as strong as Abel but I can do most of the things he docs round the farm. I can do the milking with Bill, and I could take the churns up to the road, if he'd lift them into the trap for me."

Mr. Jones looked at me. I had thought, earlier on, that he seemed sadder than usual, but now his brown eyes were not sad at all. There was a flash of white teeth under his long, thick moustache. If I hadn't know Mr. Jones better, I would have thought he was laughing.

He said, "We'd best be getting on. I reckon there's a storm coming."

Mr. Jones always knew about weather. The sky was a hot, deep blue, no clouds anywhere, but by the time we had finished the field the thunder was crackling all round the valley and the birds had stopped singing.

It was a lovely, wild evening; black as pitch except when the lightning sheeted the sky and turned the hills white. Around midnight the wind began, and rain battered the windows like bullets. Then the wind dropped and the rain became so solid and heavy that it leaked through the roof and into the apple room from the attic, bulging and soaking the ceiling and showering down plaster. James and I lugged our camp beds into Abel's room, and found his bed empty. It was five o'clock in the morning.

We got into Abel's bed; a big brass bed with a

soft feather mattress that billowed about us. We meant to stay awake, to find out what had happened, but we were too warm and comfortable. We were fast asleep when Abel came back; we only woke up when he crawled in between us, icy cold, shivering.

He had been up most of the night with the pony. She had been alarmed by the storm and tried to get out of the field through a gap in the hedge that had been roughly mended with wire. Abel and Mr. Jones had found her snaggled up by the barbed wire, torn and bleeding, with her newborn foal dead beside her.

T E N

The pony had been put in the loose box. Her head hung; she was trembling; all her skin twitching. One foreleg was badly torn; you could see the white bone. But she stood fairly still while Abel sponged the wound gently, murmuring soothing words to her. Although she had rolled frightened eyes at me, it wasn't until Mr. Jones came into the stall that she began to jerk frantically, backing away, kicking over the bucket of disinfectant, crashing against the sides of the loose box.

Abel crooked his arm round her neck, holding her head tight against him, murmuring lovingly, "It's all right, old girl, hush now, my beauty."

Mr. Jones bent to look at her leg. Abel watched him. He went on talking to Angel but his eyes were fixed on his father.

Mr. Jones straightened up. He said, "Not much help for that. Not that I can see. Sorry, lad."

"She'll mend," Abel said. "Let me get the vet, Dad."

Mr. Jones shook his head. "Waste of money. She'll be lame. Good for nothing. A bullet is kinder."

"She'll be all right as a brood mare," Abel said. "Earn her keep that way."

Mr. Jones looked at him. Their eyes met. It was as if a rope stretched tautly between them. Mr. Jones said, "Breeding horses isn't my business."

"I'll look after her," Abel said. "I'll do everything."

There was a long silence. Mr. Jones chewed the ends of his moustache. At last he said slowly, "Months. It'll take months 'fore she's healed. Think on that."

Abel sighed; a huge sigh, as if all the breath was being squeezed out of him. I saw his throat move, his Adam's apple bobbed up and down as he swallowed. Then he nodded and Mr. Jones shrugged his shoulders. "Epsom salts and hot water," he said. "A good soaking twice a day. That'll clean the pus out. And give her some hot mash. Keep her strength up."

When he had gone, Abel gave a long whistle. He said, "Strikes a hard bargain, my dad. I'd have been off to Uncle Josh, end of next week, if it wasn't for Angel."

I said, "Was he really going to shoot her? That's awful."

Abel grinned. "Merciful, that's how he'd see it. He don't like to see animals suffer. No more do I, but life's worth a bit of pain. I mean, we think it's worth it." Turning solemn, he tipped his cap back and scratched at his head. "Funny, though! I'd put an old dog out of its misery, not think twice about it. But horses is different somehow. I wouldn't want to send Angel off before her proper time, any more than I would my old mam."

He stopped short and frowned. The color rushed into his face. I knew he wished he hadn't said that, so I said quickly, to help him, "Or a cousin, or something."

For a second he stared at me. Then he gave a sudden, loud shout of laughter. "You gone a bit cracked this morning? How many cousins you got with four legs and a tail?"

"All animals are our cousins in a way," our mother said. "Very distant, of course, but it's a scientific fact, all the same. Monkeys are our closest relations, the most obvious ones, anyway, but if you think about it,

95

study the theory of evolution, you'd find we had something in common with all living creatures."

Charlie bit his bottom lip and growled fiercely, "My cousin's a saber-toothed tiger."

James giggled. "More likely an elephant, I'd say, the way you go lumbering about. You'd only have to pull your nose long enough, it might grow into a trunk."

"You're a pig without doing anything," Charlie said crossly. "Just a pig. A horrible, mean, piggy pig."

"Pigs aren't mean," I said. "Pigs are nice animals."

Charlie snorted. "Not when you've got a nasty rude one for a brother."

"Don't be silly," our mother said. "What I'm telling you has got nothing to do with pigs and elephants *now*. Just that millions and millions of years ago we all had the same ancestors. We all started life in the sea and then developed along different ways. Talking about cousins is a bit muddling, perhaps. But it's a way of explaining why it's natural for people to feel a kind of kinship with animals. Why Abel feels the way he does about horses. It's a kind of instinct inside him that makes him horse-minded."

"Like Mr. Jones is sheep-minded and we're squirrel-minded," James said. He was playing boxing with Henry, pummeling his white stomach with his doubled fist. This was Henry's favorite game; he asked for it by standing on his hind legs, quite still, waiting for James to punch him, his head on one side as if he were listening for the bell to announce the next round.

"I wish Henry were my real cousin," Charlie said. "I wish he were my real *brother*."

He sounded wistful. I said, "He's near enough, near as he can be. I mean, he's one of our *family*."

"I hope Dad will think so," James said. "I hope he likes Henry."

"I hope Henry likes *Dad*," Charlie said.

I knew what he was thinking. Henry liked people. He had only once been unfriendly. There was a rich bachelor farmer who sometimes brought presents for us; fresh salmon, ripe peaches, pheasants and partridge in season. James and I thought that he was in love with our mother, but he was so shy that he usually left the presents with Mrs. Jones and went away without seeing her. If she happened to be at the window she would call out her thanks, or run down to ask him if he would like to come in for a cup of tea, but he always said no, until this one time. He came up to our room, crimson with shyness, puffing his pipe. And Henry had hated him instantly. He flew about the room chattering with rage; then retreated to his nest on the top of the bookcase and heaved around in it, swearing furiously, *Vut, vut, vut,* all the time the poor man was there. It was because he was smoking a pipe, our mother had said, but James had told

Charlie and me that he thought it was because Henry didn't care for strange men.

"Dad will be a strange man to Henry," Charlie said.

He meant that Dad would be a strange man to *him*. The color came and went in his face as it often did when he thought about Dad coming home. He knew what Dad looked like; he had a photograph of him in his naval uniform with "To Charlie with love" written across it, but it wasn't the same as remembering him in his mind.

And that scared him.

Our mother said, "Dad and Henry will get on like a house on fire. Don't worry, Charlie."

Charlie scowled and kicked at the table leg. Our mother smiled. "Henry's more likely to be upset by all those young hooligans you've asked to your birthday party. You'll have to tell them to be quiet until he gets used to them. We don't want him frightened."

Charlie's scowl disappeared. He said scornfully, "Henry won't be frightened! He's the bravest squirrel in the whole world! He's so brave he's more like a *lion*. And he's looking forward to my party!"

Charlie had invited eight boys; one guest for each year of his life. The year before he had asked three girls and four boys, but this year he said he had grown out of girls because they didn't like fighting. "No fighting games indoors, *if* you please," our mother said, and so they played in the orchard until it started to rain and then they came storming up the stairs, shouting. "Don't frighten Henry," our mother told them, but Charlie was right: Henry wasn't scared in the least.

In fact, he had never been so excited. He showed off; snatching food from the table, hurrying to tuck it away in the curtain frills, dashing back for more, tearing up and down the curtains faster and faster, until they swung right out into the room. When James and I organized games, blindman's bluff and passing the parcel, Henry joined in, flying from one head to another and playing hide-and-seek and catch-me-if-you-can, having the time of his life among all these rowdy little trees that had suddenly turned up to play with him. He did his toffee trick and his strip-the-pencil trick, and everyone cheered him.

"Don't know about Henry, but I'm exhausted," James said, when they all went, clumping down the stairs, and we helped our mother clear up the mess.

But Henry wasn't tired. Later on, after Charlie had gone to bed, I went into the kitchen. I thought Henry was asleep in the pocket of our mother's old coat on the back of the door, and I was as quiet as I could be, putting the kettle on the oil stove to make tea, but his head popped up instantly. I turned my

back, pretending that I didn't know he was there, and waited for him to land on the top of my head or my shoulder. Instead, something new and strange happened. Usually you could hear him quite plainly as he hopped about, his little padded feet making firm *thumps* as they landed, but tonight he made no sound at all. He wasn't just quiet; he was absolutely silent. If I hadn't managed to catch sight of his tiny shadow flitting from one patch of dark to the other, I wouldn't have known he was there.

I stood very still, holding my breath. At last, out of the corner of my eye, I saw him flash back into his pocket, and I crept out with the tray. I wanted to tell James and our mother that our tame squirrel had suddenly turned into a wild, shy, secret creature, but James was drawing, and Charlie was tossing about in bed and grumbling in his sleep, and our mother put her finger to her lips to warn me not to wake him. So I poured her tea and gave her a biscuit and sat beside her, leaning against her, and started to think about going back to school next week, and saying good-bye to everyone, and although I didn't mind going back to school, really, I began to feel sad. I whispered, "I wish I was at the beginning again. It's been the best holidays ever, the best summer of my whole life," and I heard her sigh.

She stroked the back of my neck with her finger and said, "Then you've got something that no one can take away from you. Something good to remember."

ELEVEN

When I came home for the Christmas holidays, the first thing I saw was the cage. It wasn't a proper cage, just a wooden frame with chicken wire stretched across it that cut off a corner of the room from the floor to the ceiling. There was a big tree branch inside it. I said, "What's that for? Henry hates cages."

I saw James look at our mother. She said quickly, "Oh, he's not often in it. And it's not to keep him in, more to keep certain people *out*. Some of Charlie's friends can be a bit rough sometimes."

I thought of Henry at Charlie's party. I said, "That's not true. Henry loves to play, he loves people. How long has it been there? Why didn't you tell me?"

I was hot with rage suddenly; my coming-home anger. It seemed that whenever I went away they closed a door in their minds and forgot all about me. I said, "You never tell me anything. You didn't even tell me Mrs. Jones was dead until a week after!"

"There was a lot to do," our mother said. "I wrote as soon as I had a minute. Oh, I suppose I put it off a bit. I knew how upset you would be. And there was nothing . . ."

"You didn't want me to come home for the funeral," I said bitterly. "James went, and Charlie, but you didn't want me. . . ."

I hadn't thought of this before and I didn't really believe it now; I said it because it was the nastiest thing I could think of.

"That's not fair!" James said. "We were just *here,* that's why we went to the funeral. There was no point in dragging you back, spending all that money on fares! Mum and I talked about it a lot and *both* decided. . . ."

"Behind my back!" I said. "Without asking me!"

"There wasn't *time.* Letters take ages. Mum did think she might ring the school and ask to speak to you, but the telephone at the shop was out of order, and you know how far it is up to the public one on the Bent Hill. You're just being *horrible.*"

"That'll do, James," our mother said. "She's unhappy about Mrs. Jones, don't make it worse for her." She put her arms round me and hugged me. She said in a gentle voice, "I know how sad you are, darling."

I started to cry and although to begin with I was more angry than sad—angry about the cage, angry because James had called me horrible, and angry because I knew I was horrible—as I thought about Mrs. Jones dying, gone forever and ever, the sadness rose up in my throat and made me cry harder.

Our mother sat down and I sat on her lap and she pressed my face into her shoulder. I was still wearing my school uniform and my hat tipped back, and the tight elastic dug into my neck, but it was comforting to be held like that, like a baby, and so I didn't complain. She let me go after a bit and gave me a handkerchief to blow my nose, and said, "No one could have wanted her to go on living, she was in such pain at the end and so weary. But she was a lovely, brave person. We shall all miss her."

I saw tears in her eyes. There were other people she knew in the country, but no one she saw every day as she had seen Mrs. Jones, no other best friend her own age to talk to. She was lonely in that way, though not as lonely as I'd been at school when the letter came about Mrs. Jones and there was no one to talk to about it. I felt sorry for myself, remembering how I had felt with no one around me who knew her. At least our mother had had James and Charlie.

And, of course, Henry.

He had been taking a nap in his nest. He woke

and came leaping down, chattering. He ran all over me, smelling my skin, nibbling my ear, tickling the back of my neck. I had bought some peppermint creams on my sweet ration; I gave him one and he jumped onto the mantelpiece with it and straddled his legs wide to balance himself as he stuffed it into his mouth with both hands. He looked awkward like that; more like a small kangaroo than a squirrel.

"He's greedy for sweets," James said. "Just like Charlie."

I took off my silly school hat and skimmed it across the room. It landed on a chair upside down and Henry, who had finished his peppermint cream, sailed off the mantelpiece and landed inside it. I said, "Where *is* Charlie?"

"Gone off with Mr. Jones, round the sheep," our mother said. "You know I wrote and told you I thought he'd be miserable when Mario went back to the camp? Well he was, for a bit, but Mr. Jones took him off to town with him the next market day, and now Charlie sticks to him close as a shadow."

Charlie was a bit of a turncoat, I thought. I said, "*I'm* sorry that Mario's gone. I don't like things changing."

"Oh, you can't stop the world turning," our mother said. She laughed. "Will you just *look* at that squirrel!"

Henry was going backward up the curtain with

my hat, holding it in his mouth by the elastic. The hat bobbed up and down as he made the leap from the curtain top to the picture frame and from there to the top of the bookcase. His nest was huge now; twice the size it had been when I left at the end of the summer. And Henry was larger and even more beautiful; his dark red coat shone. "His adult coat," our mother said. "He's really grown up now!"

Henry wasn't the only one who had grown. James was taller, and I was both taller and thinner; when I got out of my school uniform and put on my farm clothes, my old jodhpurs, bleached pale with washing, were looser round my waist than I remembered, and shorter in the leg.

But Abel had grown most of all.

When I went down to the yard, he was turning in from the lane, sitting high on the heavy, green Fordson tractor. He shouted, "I've been waiting on you all day. Thought you mightn't be coming," and his voice cracked, swooping from high to low. He parked the tractor in the wagon shed and jumped down. He wasn't just taller. He looked different altogether; more like a man than a boy.

I said, "The train was late and I had to get the afternoon bus. I didn't know you were allowed on the tractor."

"Someone's got to do a bit of old plowing," he said. "Dad's rheumatics plague him in this sharp weather." He took a cigarette out of his cap and lit it.

I said, "I'm sorry."

He narrowed his eyes and stared over my shoulder. "It's something old men have to get used to."

Although I was sorry about Mr. Jones's rheumatism, of course, it wasn't what I had meant, and I guessed Abel knew it. But his face had gone shuttered and shy, and I gave up trying to say I was sorry about his mother. I said, "I'm sorry you didn't get to go and work for your uncle. If that's what you wanted."

He drew on his cigarette, and coughed. He said, "I reckoned Uncle Josh could get along without me. Dad can't manage just with old Bill. If he could have kept Mario on, it might've been different. But you need a woman in the house to see to the cooking, and that. It's army regulations to provide proper meals if you have a prisoner. And Dad didn't fancy a housekeeper. He says him and me and Bill on our own, we can manage."

I thought—if only he'd gone to his uncle when his mother had wanted him to, as soon as the harvest was over! I said, "How's the white pony?"

She was in the chicken field. We stood at the gate and Abel called to her. She came at a clumsy run, limping dot-and-go-one; several times her injured leg almost gave way beneath her. I said, "She's very lame, isn't she? Will she get any better?"

He was stroking her nose, giving her an apple core he had in his pocket. "Pretty well good for nothing," he said. But he sounded perfectly cheerful. He looked at me, blue eyes very bright. "She'll not be quite useless, though. You need a nursemaid for a young horse. Come and look in the stables."

I could hear the horse snorting and stamping as we got close but as soon as I saw him, I knew there was no need to be nervous; he was only restless because he was lonely. He came up to us as soon as we went in the loose box, whinnying softly, and stood still while we patted him. He was twice the size of Angel; a brown gelding with a white patch on his forehead and one white fetlock. Abel hadn't named him yet. He called him the hunter, though he said that he hadn't been bred to jump fences. "Dad bought him for the trap, really. But he's young for that. First thing is, get him used to the saddle."

The hunter had never been ridden. Abel put him in the field with Angel and he frisked about joyfully, bucking and throwing up his back legs. When he was quieter, Angel hobbled up to him and he blew down his nose to greet her, and then trotted away, looking back from time to time as if he knew she was lame and would find it hard to keep up with him. "He'd pine without company," Abel said. "And old Angel will teach him to come when he's called. If she wasn't there, I'd never get near him."

The next couple of days, every spare minute he had, Abel worked on the horse. He coaxed him into a bridle. He ran him around in a circle on the end of a rope. He talked to him lovingly. I sat on the chicken-field gate, watching him, and sometimes Mr. Jones came to watch, too. He didn't say anything, but I saw him smile behind his moustache. I wondered if he had bought the horse to cheer Abel up after Mrs. Jones died. Or if it had been meant as a bribe. "A bit of both, probably," our mother said. "And if you're going to hang about doing nothing while Abel breaks in that horse, you'd better put on an extra thick sweater."

It was bright, cold winter weather; a skin of ice on the puddles, and the grass so stiff with frost in the mornings that the blades cracked underfoot. "Going to be a berry winter," Mr. Jones said, and the hips and haws were already bright in the hedgerows. "I hope it snows for Christmas," Charlie said.

Christmas was two weeks away. We hadn't heard when our father was coming. But the telephone at the shop had been mended and our mother had had a message to ring a number in Shrewsbury. One of our father's American friends had been drafted into

the army and was stationed there. He had a letter
from our father for us and a big parcel that was too
heavy and awkward to send through the post. Our
mother was going to Shrewsbury to collect it. We
knew from her smile that she knew what was in the
parcel, but she wasn't telling. She said, "It's a present
for all of us, in a way, but it's mostly for Charlie, so
I'm taking him with me."

Charlie was up very early. He put on his best
clothes, his gray flannel suit and his smartest white
shirt, and he polished his shoes several times over.
He couldn't eat breakfast. He hopped up and down
while our mother took off one hat and put on another. At the last moment he decided that he needed
to go to the privy. I said, "Hurry up, Charlie, or you'll
be late," only meaning to tease him, but he turned
pale with terror.

James and I walked them to the bus. Charlie was
too excited to speak. When we got to the stop, he
saw a speck of mud on one shoe and his face crum-
pled up. I knelt and rubbed it off with my handkerchief and he managed a watery smile. Then, as the
bus came round the corner and stopped with a hissing
of brakes, his eyes grew round with a new anxiety. "I
forgot to say good-bye to Henry!"

"We'll say good-bye for you," James said. When
the bus had gone, he winked at me. "What a fuss!
It's all because of Dad, really. Charlie's dead scared
Dad won't like him."

"It's one of Dad's *friends* that he's meeting. This American major. Not Dad."

"I suppose Charlie thinks he might write to Dad, say what a horrible boy your son is. Something like that."

I felt a bit sad for Charlie. I tried to think how he was feeling. I said, "It's as if Dad was some sort of ogre to him. Like in a fairy tale."

James laughed. I said, "It's not *funny*. Not funny to Charlie! I mean, if he's all dark and scared about Dad in his mind. I mean, you'd need some kind of magic way of explaining. Some sort of sign!"

James pulled one of his faces. "It'll be all right once Dad's home. What's more important is, we've got to talk about Christmas presents. I've got four pounds and twelve shillings saved up."

I didn't have as much as that, of course. James was a much better saver than I was. But he was in a generous mood and we didn't squabble as we walked home. We filled our pockets with rose hips for Henry. Everyone on the farm had been collecting nuts all the autumn; enough to feed a whole troop of squirrels, James said.

There was no need to hurry back. Except for washing the breakfast dishes, we had left everything tidy. We stopped by Price's farm on the main road to see the new litter of piglets, and Mrs. Price called us into her kitchen and gave us freshly made Welsh cakes, dripping with butter. We stayed about half an hour there, and another half hour or so in the shop at the end of our lane, looking for Christmas presents. We brought a pretty comb for our mother to put in her hair, and a beautiful blue powder puff made of swansdown, and a horn penknife for Charlie. Then, as we passed the mill by the brook, Mrs. Morgan opened the door and beckoned us in. She had just made her first batch of mince pies and had packed up a tin for Mr. Jones and Abel and Bill. There were plenty left over, she said. I ate six. I don't know how many James ate, but it can't have been as many as that, because when Mrs. Morgan said she was just about to put the men's lunch on the table and we were welcome to stop, since she knew that our mother had gone off to Shrewsbury, he accepted at once. Mrs. Morgan was the best cook in the world, and she had made a rabbit stew with dumplings and herbs that smelt wonderful. But I was too full, and I didn't want to start getting fat again.

It had turned warmer since midday. The ice had gone from the puddles, and the wind had got up; a skittish, blustery wind that bent the tall hedges and sent the clouds racing. As I trudged up the lane, I could see Henry in the chicken-field window; a red blob, very small, very still.

I thought he looked lonely, and that made me feel guilty. It was the third day of the holidays and I had been so busy, I hadn't once played with him properly, or taken him out. "I'm back, Henry," I

called, when I opened the door. "I'm sorry we left you so long," and he jumped on me and dived in my pocket after the rose hips. I fed him nuts after that, and put a saucer of milk on the windowsill. I laid the table for supper, and filled the oil lamps, and washed the breakfast mugs and the porridge plates, using the last of the water.

I picked up the empty buckets. Henry had finished his lunch and was sitting quiet on the sill, watching the wind. His arms were folded across his chest. Like an old man, dreaming.

I said, "Come on, you lazy squirrel," and he flew to my shoulder.

Outside, the day was darkening a little, but in a nice, just-before-Christmas way; the sky bellied with what might be snow, and the wind whipped the trees in the orchard, blowing the last leaves off the black branches. It was perfect weather for Henry. He tore aloft, from one tree to another, swooping, tumbling with the falling leaves, faster and faster; as excited as he had been at Charlie's party, only these were real trees, tossing in the wild air.

I watched for a while, until I began to get chilly. I called him, but he didn't come; just stopped for a second to play hide-and-seek with me round the trunk of a tree. Then he darted up higher.

And that was the last I saw of him; a flash of reddy gold light, against the dark sky.

James said, "We don't take him out anymore. That's why we built the cage. To put him in when the windows were open."

"But he always came back!"

"They got scared he might not. Mum and Charlie."

"Why didn't you *tell* me he wasn't allowed out of doors any longer?"

"You didn't ask!"

"I didn't know that I needed to. We always took him out. All the summer."

"It was after you'd gone back to school that we stopped. We'd got so *fond* of him. . . ."

"I'm fond of him, too. That's why I took him out, I thought he wanted to play. It seemed mean to leave him shut up alone in the house. And I had all these tidying up things to do! *You* weren't here to help, were you? Stuffing your greedy face at the mill. And he was having such a good time. I thought I'd just fetch the water. And I stopped to talk to Abel a bit, and watch him with the horse. But we'd left Henry in the orchard before."

"Don't cry," James said. "Perhaps he'll come back."

I said, "What will Mum say? And *Charlie?*"

T W E L V E

Charlie thundered up the stairs, the parcel clutched to his chest. He plonked it on the table and tore off the paper. Three polished, round wooden lids; three different sizes, each with a brass handle.

Charlie said, "They're for the privy. A big lid, and a medium lid, and a little lid. To put on the holes and stop the wind blowing the paper."

James and I looked, saying nothing. Charlie was so excited, spit flew from his mouth. "I wrote to Dad, and Dad wrote to Mum, and Mum sent the measurements, and Dad got the ship's carpenter to make them for me. It's the best present I've ever had, the best present of my whole life! Dad had them made for me, just for *me*. And he'll be home Christmas Eve, and his friend, Major Harper, Major Cass Harper, says he'll be proud when he sees me, how much I've grown. He said, Major Harper said, he wished he'd got a boy like me to come home to!"

His eyes sparkled; his whole face was lit, as if a lamp shone inside him. He was fizzing with happiness. James and I looked at him, and then at our mother, and in the silence that followed Charlie looked at the three of us, slowly turning his gaze from one to the other. And our mother said, softly and very reluctantly, "What's happened? Where's Henry?"

We looked for him until late that night. Mr. Jones came, and Abel, and Bill, and we had lanterns and torches. The moon was full; a pearly globe sailing between tattered clouds. We searched the orchard, and the fields, and the lane, and the barn. Charlie started to stumble with weariness, and Bill picked him up and carried him high on his shoulder. "Henry," we called, and the wind seemed to lift his name and blow it away. At last, our mother said, "I expect he's fast asleep in a nice hollow tree. You know how he hates to stay up past his bedtime."

And so we went home. James went to sleep quickly, but I stayed awake for a long time and listened to the wind sighing round the old house and through the attics over my head as if it were looking for something. It seemed a friendly sort of wind, and I tried to think about Henry, curled up warm and safe somewhere. But I ached inside.

Our mother said, talking to Charlie, to comfort him, but talking to the rest of us, too; to James and me and our father, "We were lucky to have had him so long. And he was well fed and healthy and smart enough to find his own food and a good place to hole up for the winter. You just think of him, finding a mate and raising a family and telling his children how much things have changed since he was a young squirrel. How there used to be nice, soft things like knickers and socks lying around to build nests with, and useful trees that grew nuts and fruit at all seasons."

She looked across the room at our father and smiled, and he smiled back, and I wondered if they were thinking about James and Charlie and me growing up and leaving home, just like Henry.

Charlie said, "What'll we do with all Henry's nuts? Shall we eat them?"

And that is the end of Henry's story; all that I know for sure, anyway. Abel said, the week after Christmas, that he had seen a squirrel in the tree by the brook and it hadn't run away when he cantered past on the hunter, just sat there calmly and looked at him. He said, "I reckon he can take care of himself, your old squirrel."

I kept a good watch on that tree and, although I didn't see Henry, I lost the ache in my chest and started to think of him living happy and free.